I0549465

AMERICAN SLAVE

ROMAN
DRAKE

Movement Publishing House

This is a work of fiction. All of the characters, organizations, and events portrayed in this novel are either products of the author's imagination or are used fictitiously.

Copyright © 2009 by Roman Drake

All rights reserved. No part of this book may be reproduced in any form by any means without the prior written consent of the Publisher, excepting brief quotes used in reviews.

Library of Congress Catalog Card Number: 2013905999

ISBN: 0939259307

Printed in the United States of America
10 9 8 7 6 5 4 3 2 1

ISBN 13: 978-0989259309

Berkeley, CA

www.movementpublishinghouse.com

ACKNOWLEDGMENTS

Thank you to my friend, who inspired the character Richard. To my father, for always being there. Kristy Jordan, for helping me discover who I was, before, during, and after writing this book. My publishing, and creative team, for answering all of my naive questions and never making me think I was stupid. A big thank you to a summer job I had in Indiana, that made me walk through a hundred and ten degree ovens for a whole day before I quit.

Hello, my name is Richard G. Wright, I'm the nobody working behind the cash register that you forget to give the common courtesy of sharing eye contact with, right before you hand me a hard-earned fifty for your maternity clothes, if you're daring enough to be in the position to need them. We share this common bond amongst us nobodies, we all like to think we are somebody, or that we could be somebody, giving us the pleasure of eye contact from other human beings. I think it's hope that gives us this delusion, in my opinion hope is man's greatest curse, that's what keeps people like me going. Things are forever changing though, nothing stays the same, but in this moment of my life, it seemed that this world would never end.

Yeah, I'm the regular nobody working at a bullshit job, I have a stupid little workforce vest on, with my long hair tied up and put in a bun -- yes it's silky, I use Herbal Essences. Some people at first glance would guess that I have some Hispanic blood in me, but this is false, I have some distant Cherokee blood that has given me a tanned complexion. For the most part, people know I'm white; I live in Indianapolis, Indiana. Though, every once in awhile there will be some inbred, four-wheelin', dirt-bike-riding hillbilly who will treat me like a Mexican working alongside them at a factory. I'm not a fucking Mexican.

I work at an up-and-coming maternity clothing store in Indiana, which for legal reasons I will refer to as the bullshit job, or the shitty job. I've watched it grow in the last few years with the success of opening up other stores around Indiana, making me want to hyperventilate. At the moment I'm masturbating with my hand in my pocket behind the counter, watching a plump twenty-three-year old MILF shop for her baby girl's diapers, I can already see her trying to decide which kind she should buy -- the cheap kind or the well advertised brand name? Both are the same, one just has the illusion of being better because of its stupid commercials on prime-time television. I have this thing I do when I close my eyes, I think no one else can see me, that's what I was doing when this twenty-three-year old MILF came up to me. "Excuse me, but are you jacking off?" she asked.

I opened my eyes and thought, *Yes, exactly what you should have made the retard who came inside you do, what idiot would forget to pull out of a white trailer-trash skank like this?* "No," I said. The deep mascara along with the over-fried dyed hair really had me going, so I closed my eyes and pretended like she wasn't there, at least until I finished, which isn't that long usually.

"What are you doing? Are you serious right now? You're still doing it? You're masturbating, aren't you?" she asked.

"Nah," I replied as I finished, opened my eyes, and took my hand out of my pocket at the same time, like nothing happened. "If I were masturbating, I'd be looking at a Martha Stewart picture in the bathroom, I'm not stupid enough to be masturbating out here."

She looked at me with a dumbfounded look only someone like her could. "Don't let me catch you looking like that in front of my baby girl again!"

I was sure I would see her baby daughter twenty years from now buying baby clothes for her daughter as I, forty-something, would still be standing behind the same counter, rubbing one off at the sight of her. "Sorry." I explained, "I didn't get much sleep last night."

She walked away and I stood there wishing I could slap her in the face with the meat between my legs. The only reason I didn't was because I really needed this assistant manager position at the store, all signs were pointing to Steven Schram getting it. He's a preppy kiss-ass I couldn't stand with Eminem-wannabe dyed-blonde hair. This fucking company is making millions of dollars while we make pennies, and this fucker would take less if they asked him to. Why the hell anyone would bend over backwards for a job like this is beyond me, but the reason I need it is so I can get my own place.

Markus, my high school buddy, co-worker, and roommate, was really starting to get on my nerves. Living together sounded like a good idea at first, we both wanted a cheap place, but our house looked more like a crack house. In fact, that's what we called it. It's pretty much what a crack house would be like, only with IKEA-decorated, after-college accessories. The carpets looked like someone puked on them after they had finished eating root beer floats. The walls were yellow, probably from smokers before us. The house hadn't really been redone since the forties, that's how the last tenant kept it until she died. I always wondered if she had died in the bathtub. The stains at the bottom of the tub looked as if she had died and sat there for a few weeks before anyone realized it. Aside from old junkies knocking on our door on random nights looking for one last nosedive, Markus was the main problem. He wouldn't flush the toilet when he pissed, would leave the door open when he masturbated, and actually had a direction for his life. The last one pissed me off the most. He was a D student in high school, I was on the A and B honor roll every semester, and somewhat cool and popular too, but nothing like this fuck stain Steve and his preppy robots. Markus fucked around, looked at all the girls' asses instead of finishing his tests. We both smoked the Mary Jay on weekends but I didn't smoke like this fucking tard, he was an idiot, I had to light the pipe for him all the fucking time because he couldn't do it himself. Really, if you know what I'm talking about, it's not that hard. This Markus, though, he's gonna head off to California, probably fucking do something with his life. He was a natural sex machine, and as cliché as it sounds, his cock was pretty big too, not that I'm a fag or anything but this guy fucked girls nonstop, made 'em bleed all over the sheets a few times too. I know this 'cause I lost a bet over the super bowl between the Colts and the Saints -- I washed his sheets and asked him about it. He was making a porno, with a football theme; he called it "Anal Spiking". I still have nightmares, he made me watch the thing though and I have to say, he's the Roman Polanski of porn. Markus knew everything about porn, too -- the directors, the actors and actresses; he'd sit and watch the shit so much a woman's vagina stopped making me get hard. I even started having my own personal favorites. Tory Lane was one crazy bitch, when I watched her she made me grow wood faster then Johnny Appleseed, but after I came, I couldn't help to wonder about her own personal safety, she made me wonder what it would be like to gang-bang a girl, and I think that had an effect on what I'd do later. Markus never worked out, but he looked like Brad Pitt in that movie "Troy". He ate more than me, too, which really pissed me off. I'm not fat, but I can have a weight problem or two if I eat the shit Markus eats. You see, the thing that made Markus a somebody, was that he actually believed in porn, not as just a career but as a life. He would spout off for hours if you let him about the oppression religion has put on sex and how it was his duty to make the most original and best sex movies possible, so that people who were too scared to show their true side in everyday life could show their true side in the bedroom, their animal self, the natural being that everyone is. It was actually inspiring to hear him talk, sometimes I felt like his fucking would one day save the world. Somebody needed to. The truth was I was jealous of his direction and passion, I wish I had it myself; I wish there was something I wanted as bad as Markus.

Me, though, I don't know. Sometimes I felt like I was drowning. It was when I went up for air -- that's when All the pain would hit me, that's when the drama of life comes at you full force, when you're drowning, it's only about whether or not you'll make it, whether or not you'll survive, that's how it should be. Lately, I wish I had the guts to see what was on the other side, it couldn't be any worse than life. I'm naked and under my own bath water when Markus walks in and begins peeing in the toilet. I watch, holding my breath begins to become too hard. Typical, he doesn't flush and walks out. I come up, gasping for air. Life could be made easy if there was an on and off switch. I wanted to be turned off indefinitely, sometimes.

I'm outside of a small fenced-in rental home that could be more like a two-fifty-a-month home instead of the four hundred they're asking. My blonde, not too skanky, Abercrombie-wearing girlfriend stands in front of me, slapping her hands together in excitement. This is Veronica, she's the type of girl who was picked on too much in middle school, she has to make up for it by trying to get the attention of every man in a five-mile radius by wearing clothes so tight you can see the curve of her lips. No, I'm not talking about the lips on her face. What happened to the national speedometer of women's self esteem? I see it All over the place, women wearing tight things like they're on a sexual display. Veronica changes her hair color every few weeks to the next slutty "IN" thing that will grab attention. She doesn't know what she wants either, just like me, but often we thinks we do. Right now it's playing house with me so she can pretend we're moving toward marriage like All her other friends are doing right now. Me and Veronica are the typical naive couple that has been dating since high school.

"This could be our first place, can you believe it?" She can't.

"No, I really can't," I unenthusiastically reply.

"You don't like it?" she asks.

"Not really," I reply.

She tries to entice me. "We could have a lot of sex in here."

"Well, we can have a lot of sex in the Ford Explorer here too, and I already own the Ford Explorer," I reply as I point to my SUV.

She pouts. "Be serious." The fact is that I am a terribly lonely person, but it's a love-hate relationship I have with being lonely. People can't hurt you if you're alone, they can't lie to you, they can't tell you what they really think of you, even though at this point I wish Veronica would, it would be a lot better than this fake face she's been giving me the last few years. It was when we started getting comfortable with each other, that was when her shrewdness started to show, we stopped having sex as much and I was deprived, far enough that I found myself begging for it, like a Labrador wanting to get inside the house. Instead of smiling when she was around me, she started having a face of frustration. Relationships are so good at the beginning. There's the movies, the going out to eat with conversations that are new, it's somewhat fun getting to know the person that they are showing you, and it's fun to let the other person think they know you, but the truth is, you never really know anyone, just fragments of them. The fragments they don't show you come out later, sometimes on accident, sometimes in arguments, sometimes when suspecting them of wanting to fuck your best friend and roommate, Markus. You see, even if she hasn't, I knew she wanted to. The look is unmistakable; I used to get the look. Now Markus gets the look, the flirting that's so subtle someone outside the relationship would call you a maniac, but you know, all guys know. Like the way Veronica plays with her hair when talking to him, like she's nervous, or the way she smiles and laughs at everything he says that's not even funny. She denies it every time I mention it and she pretends to try not to do it again but it still comes out in subtle ways. Girls are like that though; they have to play silly little games all the time to raise their self-esteem. I blame it on women's oppression; not letting them vote for so long has really fucked us in the ass. I also blame it on the hippie and feminist movement, probably one of the worst things that could have happened. It didn't stop a war, it just made it OK for women to be crack whores and spread sexually transmitted diseases. More recently though, in my lifetime, it's been a change in how big business sells their products. At first it was women being objectified as sex objects everywhere, women burnt their bras, but then were somewhat shut up when they started objectifying men. Now we're forced to listen to some slut in a skimpy skirt on the Ξ Channel who has some need to let everyone know who she thinks is hot, as if the people watching wouldn't be able to decide for themselves.

So, now that the game is on, I have a game I like to play too. It's called fucking her best friend. That way as she plays her stupid little game, I play mine, except when I play, I play to win, and if you ask me, I'm winning, she just doesn't know it. It shouldn't even bother me when I think about what I've done, but when I think about what I've done, it makes me think she's out there doing something worse, so I have to up the ante. So far, I cheated once with a girl from my high school on the Fourth of July, once in my neighbor's swimming pool, once with her slutty best friend on Halloween, and once at a local rock concert with some wannabe Metallica band playing in the background. Honestly, I would love to stand there and tell her All about it, but honesty is something a female hasn't heard of. For me to do that, she would have to spill the beans about what she's been doing. I would immediately tell her after, in a fit of rage no doubt, as she stands there on the rental-home yard that is begging for someone to water it.

I think about it, but then crumble like the bastard I am. "I just don't know about playing wife and husband right now," I tell her with a face that begs her not to be mad.

She looks right back at me and says, "It's time to grow up."

I nod and think to myself, *but I don't feel grown up, at least not enough to pretend like I am.*

And that was the end of that. She got in the Ford Explorer and didn't say a word all the way back to her richie-rich father's house. She was real awkward about her family, she didn't talk much about them and I had never really formally met them, even after years of dating her. She said it was because of a middle school boyfriend that her dad had actually gotten close to. Don't ask me how a middle age man, gets attached to a kid in braces, creepy if you ask me. After they broke up her dad stated that he didn't want to know any more of her boyfriends until she was engaged. I didn't ever really know why they were rich, what he did sounded complicated, though Veronica wasn't really good at ever getting around to explaining it, or maybe she did and I had just tuned it out. She was totally uninterested in her parents; I eventually just accepted that they were rich. I can't complain though, how else do you think I would have gotten the fairly new grey Ford Explorer? Yep, got it from father on high school graduation day.

That was the day. It was June, thank God, and high school was over. It looked like nothing but the best was coming after. When you're in high school it looks dismal, but talk to any nobody four years after and they would be begging to have detention again.

My father is a private doctor; I grew up in the basement. You know you're rich when the basement you have is nicer than any of your friends' houses. I had everything I needed, bathroom, pool table, bar, big screen TV, gum ball machine. Why the hell would I go upstairs? Things were expected of me, though. They have to be when your father is a doctor. You see, the rule is that you can't fail more than your father. Markus's dad was a factory worker, big fucking mountain he has to climb. Then me, what the fuck are you supposed to do with all this time you're given? I mean, there is so much of it, lately I noticed that the forty hours at my shit job moving around boxes of maternity clothes seemed more like sixty. I hear if you do something you love, it seems like there's never enough time. College just wasn't it for me. I quit three times because I kind of had a marijuana problem. The problem wasn't that I smoked too much; I only smoked on weekends... OK, sometimes Thursdays... and every other Tuesday. The real problem was the things it made me see. Most people, they get high and they're laughing their guts out, or they're just plain happy. Not me. When I did it, things that were blurry began getting clear, too clear. Me and Markus somehow had the same experience with this. Well, maybe his was a little different. I remember that for forever he didn't think he could get high because he wasn't inhaling it right, then by some freak accident our friend Anthony lit his ass up. He started talking about "The Four Levels of Human Emotion." He said that there are four sides to life (angry, happy, sad and confused) and that all life is about as human beings are feeling these emotions. I remember he thought I was mad at him or something, but really I just wanted him to shut up about it. My mom had already found a cut-up straw in my laundry from doing coke. I told her it was for a science project, I barely made it through that, and then I had to deal with Markus's yelling about the four levels of human emotion without my parents waking up. Marijuana for me blew a spark plug I never knew I had, started making brain cells work I never thought were there, and then there were things I never really wanted or wished to see, and it made me severely depressed. I couldn't enjoy life, not that I was anyway. I couldn't see any good in it, not that I could anyway. A surprise I needed to be high for that, huh? I was at a family reunion and everyone was talking about how depressed I looked. I remember a great aunt of mine got me a shirt that actually said, "Life is Great". I couldn't believe it, I broke down, not crying or anything but I couldn't take it, I couldn't understand why anyone could see this as a good life to live. I told my father I was quitting school the next semester. My father understood and didn't cut me off until the next semester. I contemplated my life in the basement all spring and stayed away from everything green. I couldn't figure out what was wrong with life, I wasn't enjoying it like everyone else seemed to, I started to wonder if everyone was taking something that I wasn't.

I got the shitty job at the maternity clothing store and after quitting school two more times I finally landed an art history degree. Yeah, I know, a lot of good that's doing me. I thought for a time that I wanted to be curator; I spent a lot of time at the Museum of Modern Art in Indianapolis. I was drawn to the exhibits they had on slaves, the brutality seemed current even today, but not on a physical level, on an emotional level. The whips weren't being lashed out on my back, but on my mind, I didn't quite realize it then, I couldn't express it. I didn't realize a lot of things then, I didn't realize that deep down I cared for my girlfriend, Veronica, and that deep down she was a somebody, somebody who deserved a hell of a lot better than me, someone who deserved better than what I was about to do to her. The reason I wanted to be a curator was because there was something about the slavery exhibits that irked me, it lacked something, the more I looked at them the more I noticed that the exhibits were closer to Disney's point of view on slavery, as if Mickey Mouse had gone through slavery. The fake figures of the slaves along with most of the exhibit seemed to have lacked money, and one of 'em even had a Jheri curl. They deserved better, they built the country, and they helped lift America to where it is today. I argued with the curator in charge and finally got an answer. Apparently the way it works now is that the museum and, as he told me, other museums he's worked for, had to bend to the people who funded the exhibits. If the people who funded the exhibits thought that the gruesome pictures of young black boys being hung should be taken down, then that's what happened, forget about the responsibility to show the black folk or what really happened. This extinguished my passion for curating later on. Funny, cause it's what sparked it, too. I kind of just gave up, realizing that when money is involved it's a lost cause.

My father never really expected me to be a doctor or anything, at least he never claimed that's what he wanted for me, but really I just wanted to make him proud. For some reason I needed to justify his twenty-two years raising me by doing something that made him proud, but lately I felt like the only thing he ever seemed to want for me was for me to have money. He nixed my idea of robbing a bank. I thought that money was what I wanted too for some time, especially in high school. I thought if I could just live in the same kind of house my father had, that would be a reason for living. Then I realized the work it took to have a house like my father had, it didn't seem worth it. My father didn't even like being a doctor, he didn't care about people or helping them, especially our older neighbor, Miss Kline. She was a hundred and seven, and rich, no one actually knew why but everyone seemed to think she got rich from killing her inventor husband. Apparently he had something to do with the wheel when it was invented. Miss Kline was always in my father's office and always claimed to be dying; everyone wondered when she would be telling the truth. My mother, who was my father's secretary at the office, said that the only thing wrong with her was that she wasn't dying and that she had the body of a fifty year old. My father was convinced that she had unfinished business still, that she was finally going to give back my father's graduation ring that he lost in her lawn while mowing it for her. My father was convinced that she found it and swiped it since she had a fascination for owning old shiny things. I could hear my father from the basement as he got home from work, he would curse her up and down and say if she ever does come in dying he won't be in any hurry to give her mouth-to-mouth.

So here I am, working, moving boxes with maternity wear for the skanks who get pregnant from a truck to my shit job warehouse. Steve, the prep, is on everyone's ass and especially mine for being five minutes late. He keeps asking me why I was late and I keep telling him I don't have a fucking answer for him. The truth was that I just didn't feel like leaving when I was supposed to, so finally I told him that. My laziness actually made him mad, I could see it in his look.

He told me, "You know why you'll be doing this forever, Richard? Because you'll have to."

Him saying this wasn't the reason I ripped up a box of maternity daisy flower clothes and threw them on top of his head, it wasn't even the constant nagging he had put me through in the last six months since him being hired. It was the fact that he was right, OK, and the fact that he thought he was better than me for getting to work early, and for doing his job beyond what was needed, and for puckering his lips up to Mr. Holden, the real boss, the one who should be on my ass but doesn't give a rat's ass about his job either. He was thirty-something years old when he was made manager; a ripe ten years later he's doing the same thing. No kids, no wife, really who can blame him. I often look at him, wondering what keeps him going. I picture him some days as a soldier storming the beaches of Normandy. That's what he is to me, a fucking hero for making it to his late forties working here without stabbing himself. If it were me I would have ended the bland existence a long time ago. That's what scared me; some days I would see how he hated his job more than me. I wondered why he was working here; I knew he started when he was in college like me. *In twenty years is that going to be me?* I thought, sighing at the sunlight creeping in on my closed shades inside my cluttered, stale-smelling office.

If something was going to happen, it needed to happen now, and quick. I needed a prayer, I needed a Hail Mary, I would have prayed myself but I had forgotten how. Mr. Holden had me and Steve in his office after he reported the incident to him like the drama queen he is. Mr. Holden was eating an apple fritter, letting the shards of sugar hit his chest without much care. Me and Steve were sitting on the side of the desk, both perturbed at each other.

Mr. Holden talked as he chewed. "Boys, one day you're gonna think of this as your prime days. They are, too, 'cause it won't get better than this. Now, what I think the two of you need is to hug. I told both of you on occasion I'm a Kentuckian, there we hug men, we hug men without shame. Here in Indiana you think it's gay to hug. I'd hug my bank teller if I knew I didn't have to worry about getting arrested."

And so we got up and hugged, awkwardly. A week later he promoted Steve as the assistant manager, surprise, surprise. Now, the extra hundred dollars I would be making per week will no longer be there. I could barely survive on the pay I was making; I didn't buy anything for myself, ever. I paid rent, I paid for gas, I paid for insurance and food, and then I was broke until the next paycheck. Still, somehow, I wondered what was wrong with my life. It's a horrible way to live but somehow people do it all the time. It made me wonder how the skank who caught me masturbating behind the counter did it. She couldn't have had much more then a waitress job, yet she had a kid. I wonder how she and her kid survived. It couldn't be easy. I felt bad and it didn't seem right, but there wasn't much I could do, I was invisible just like everyone else. I was in trouble myself, I needed out, I needed a change, I needed anything in the world to give me a sign, to tell me I was going to be OK and that I wasn't going to be Mr. Holden in twenty years.

On the weekend, me and Markus were having one of our annual "I'm tired of looking at your face so let's invite all of our friends and have a huge party until we are tired of their faces" event. Indianapolis isn't much of a college town like Bloomington or Lafayette, but it does have a lot of community colleges that a lot of our classmates go to for one reason or another. So, there were a lot of people we knew and many we didn't know. Me and Veronica were sitting on the futon, I was having an overwhelming moment because there were too many people in my room at one time. I'm an only child, and it's obvious in moments like this that I have only-child syndrome, if there is such a thing. If there isn't, there should be, and if it's in the dictionary there should be a picture of me next to it. The best way to explain it is that it's like being totally comfortable one moment, mostly when I'm alone, and then suddenly people who I haven't known for more than five minutes will come into the room, I'm not sure of 'em because I don't know them, so I don't know how to behave and end up being quiet and moving very little. Veronica, being with me a while now, didn't quite understand what I was going through, at least that was the way she acted. My nervousness made her nervous, she had too much to drink that night and was continuously talking to another guy as I sat there alone. He was the kind of guy who needed to buy whatever was fashionable at the time to make himself feel better so he could talk to girls like Veronica. Some people grow out of this but you could tell he was headed for a long life of doing what he was told, most people are, and in this moment, so was I. In our defense, we are all on a road of obedience, it starts from the time we can comprehend words and ends the time we lay face up in the dirt. It seemed as if my loneliness propelled her to another man. They talked for what seemed to be forever, as I grew sick of the situation. The guy didn't know me and I didn't know him, but the look on his face was unmistakable. I had it on my face when she was talking to me these ways years ago. I would have to say that I held my own better. I didn't lean back and smile like I was getting lucky tonight as much as this guy did. I saw that he could barely breathe; as if he breathed wrong she might change her mind. I was impressed; this guy actually seemed capable of making the first move. Hell, with a hundred and thirty dollar pair of shoes, you better be able to make the first move, 'cause what the hell do you buy clothes like that for? It's definitely not because you like them. It's because the world around you tells you that you stand a better chance of being screwed if you like them. Veronica was a sheep just like him. I might have been a sheep, too, but at least I knew it. Soon they left the room together, casually, as if they were getting something more to drink. She didn't even acknowledge me. I wanted to squeeze her heart dry, and then she would know I was there, and then she would know what I felt. Why do people hurt each other like this? Are we all here to make each other feel like we've been stabbed repeatedly with a rusty blade? Times like these really make me just look at it all and wonder why. Every footstep she and this guy took out of the room together as they maneuvered around the other people made feel so insignificant. Like a weight steadily falling in my stomach only to get to the bottom and churn for a bit. She deserved to know how this felt; she deserved to feel insignificant as well. I looked for her in the hall, I only saw blondes who I wish I could concentrate on now, blondes I wish I could give time, but the only thing I felt was for Veronica. The blondes were meaningless. I scoured the kitchen where the drinks were, and she wasn't there. The weight fell again but not as hard as I gather that they might be on the balcony together, although I hoped they wouldn't be. I slowly tried to compose myself in the kitchen, as I grabbed a bottle half full of vodka. I couldn't chug it, I could only read the details of the ingredients as I dreaded walking up to the balcony. I wanted to smash everyone's faces, those who were happily talking to one another with no idea what was going on inside me. I walked upstairs where I moved around people to get to the balcony at the end of the hall. As I walked down the middle of the hallway holding the vodka bottle distilled from grain in San Jose, eighty proof, with forty percent alcohol, I could see the cheap Chinese lanterns hanging outside on the balcony on both corners, a cool little piece of culture I bought to make me feel like I've been farther then the state line. They lit Veronica and this douche bag well as they leaned up against the balcony, looking out, talking. The douche bag was smiling confidently as he could tell Veronica's self-esteem must be low. Before I knew it I was standing on the balcony with them, just the three of us. Veronica turned around with a confused look on her face. In that moment I hated her more then any genocide or massive cruelty to humankind in the world.

The douche bag turned around, smoking a cigarette, another mechanism to trick the female mind into sleeping with him. His sheep face along with his sheep eyes looked at me and squinted. His mouth opened but all I could hear was a sheep's bleat.

Veronica's mouth opened and again all I could hear was more of the same, "Bahahahah."

In an instant, like a reflex you can't control, the same way a doctor hits your knee with that little elbow thing so that your leg will spring up, I bashed him with it, I bashed him with the distilled bottle of grain, eighty proof, and forty percent alcohol, from San Jose. The bottle broke into pieces as I hit him square in the nose; the only thing left was the bottleneck, which I still gripped. That instant reflex seemed to last forever as glass shattered everywhere, mostly in his face. Eyes, mouth, nose, forehead and cheeks, all stuck with glass. His nose seemed to take the worst of it as the tip seemed to have fallen off. Luckily his reflexes turned on, too, and he closed his eyes right before impact. The party full of happy-go-lucky people connecting with each other and having fun was over, and all anyone could hear was the wreck on this guy's face that he would have for years to come. Within a second of seeing the aftermath of this innocent guy's face, standing on the balcony of my inexpensive home, next to my unworthy girlfriend, I could tell that I had ruined his life so much so that the price of shoes would not matter anymore, nor the brand of his shirt, jeans or accessories. The guy was silent for a bit, making me think I had killed him, but soon the carnage of his voice echoed as far as the outskirts of our quaint neighborhood right outside of Indianapolis would take it. The deed was done, the reflex had happened, and Veronica stood there in shock as if she wasn't the doctor who was doing the testing on me.

"What are you doing?" she screamed.

I was silent, all I could do was look on as if I was unaffiliated with the incident, as if I were an outsider in a different body looking on at a person I didn't know, on a balcony I didn't know, who witnessed a young man ruin another man's life right in front of my eyes. The blood flew down the man's face like a waterfall; there was a hole in the man's eyelid as if the shard of glass from the bottle couldn't leave his face without a souvenir.

Moment's later, red and blue lights from three police cars were on my lawn. I cooperated the best I could as they asked questions neutrally as best they could. One of the cops, who was no doubt bothered by the gruesome scene, asked me to look him in the eyes as they asked questions. I was sitting in the back of the police car with my feet out the door as two of them circled me. I looked even though I didn't want to. He asked me if I felt bad about what happened here. I felt like I couldn't totally say yes, so I said nothing. He was carried out on a gurney next, he went into shock, and the fear of what would happen to him and me ran through my blood like electricity. I held up a stone face as best I could, although I knew everyone was watching me and could see the shame on my face. Markus stood back on the grass behind the cops, holding the hand of a blonde girl who I had never seen before. The shocking events of the night would no doubt work for or against Markus, as if he needed any help. She got into a car with her friends later as Markus just stood back, curious to know what had happened. Markus could have gone back upstairs with the girl, or even to her place, as I'm sure she offered, but suddenly as the police handcuffed me and put me in the car, I saw what a good friend Markus was. I could see him ask a nearby cop where they were going. Markus didn't exile me from his life as I expected him to after what I had done. I turned to look out the back of the window of the police car and saw Markus's car following the whole time, as if he didn't want me go through this alone, no matter how wrong I was in what I did.

I sat at the police station for about three hours as they questioned me and talked to me about the same thing over and over again. Time went on in this generic office with generic furniture and generic questions asked by generic police officers that outweighed the limit of what I thought any officer who wore a badge could legally weigh. I noticed a plain-clothed officer who seemed to outrank the other officers in the room. He stayed quiet for most of the time, but was the only one who seemed not to have judged me as a despicable human being based on my recent actions. The look in his eyes made me feel like he knew me or at least knew what I was going through. At one point, everyone else left and it was just me and him in the room. He sized me up with glances, sighed to break the silence and then asked me how old I was even though he knew. I told him twenty-three. He talked about how he was more careful with these sorts of things now. He started talking to me about his kid and how he looked to drugs for all the answers when he should have been looking to the Bible. This is common Indiana rhetoric. I couldn't argue with him on this point. He asked me if I did drugs and I told him honestly, not anymore. He said that it was good that I didn't. He told me how he knew that I was confused now but that later things would get clearer. He told me that I was released on bail and that since it was my first offense, if I had any hope of not going to jail, that I better start seeing an anger management counselor as soon as possible so that the judge might have leniency. I nodded and said thank you as he took me out.

I walked out, about ready to hug Markus for bailing me out. I knew that he couldn't afford this right now, and for the next few weeks I would be giving him my paycheck and washing his bloody sheets with gratitude. As the metal door that separated criminals and civilians opened, I walked out, ready to halfheartedly smile at Markus. Instead, I halfheartedly smiled at a disappointed and angry father, as well as a "Sorry for Richard" face on Markus. I couldn't be mad at Markus, he knew it would have took forever for me to pay him back, and the only way to get me out of there was for him to call my parents. Thankfully he did. I rode back with my father, silent, as Markus traveled in his car behind us. My father wasn't as angry as I thought he would be. He asked me if the guy had hit me. I said no. He asked me if the guy had made me angry and I said no. He asked me to explain it to him and I was embarrassed to say anything. I was embarrassed that I was with a girl that my parents liked, for two years now, and they didn't know how she made me feel, that my whole life just made me feel so insignificant. It was too embarrassing, all of it. I was just a regular guy just like everyone else, but I couldn't explain it, I couldn't explain what was wrong with me, because in fact on all accounts the best I could gather was that there wasn't anything wrong with me. Without a doubt I felt the way countless others have -- lost. It didn't make me special, it didn't make me entitled, it just made me another nobody. And yet, all this was about to change.

Weeks had passed and I hadn't talked to Veronica. Didn't want to, and I'm sure she didn't want to either. She knew what she was doing that night, playing a game like most girls do, because they have no self-esteem, not that I'm a prize when it comes to self-esteem, but at least I don't have to do a dog and pony show like she does all the time. I also knew that if we did talk, she would deny any responsibility for what had happened; by now she had formed a truth in her brain and that truth would make her believe that she was innocent. The usual excuse, as if she had no idea what she was doing. She would say that they were just talking and they were just friends and that she couldn't believe I had done that. For some of you this might work, and those few I feel sorry for as the trickery and games played on you by the female brain must be hard for your friends to stand. I realized later that there was no excuse for what I had done and that I should of broken the bottle on her face instead. I did think if I had, maybe then she would have finally figured out that I wasn't a toy and I was not to be messed with, and that there were consequences for her actions. I doubted she would ever learn. When she's eighty years old and has found someone dumb enough to put up with her games and settle down, she will be playing the same games in the hospice house. Her old husband dying as he watches that old bitch flirt with some other dying poor sap who thinks he's about to get lucky.

Time went on and so did work as Steve constantly angered me. Markus made me mad but not as much after the bottle-breaking incident, he didn't judge me and didn't ask many questions about it even though I knew he wanted to. He kind of just kept quiet about it, which was odd. I felt if he had done something like that I would have intruded until I had gotten every aspect of what had happened tattooed on my brain. Markus wasn't the nosey type and when it came down to it we were men, and men aren't allowed to talk about their emotions. If we did, in our society, we would be termed gay. Heaven forbid if someone thought that, right? It seemed now that I had ruined my already dismal life, with a pretty impulsive and stupid action. The kid at my party was seventeen years old, he wasn't a sheep after all, he actually had a name -- Nathan Gore. He was just some seventeen-year-old kid, drinking and talking to my older girlfriend. It was official -- I was due to pay him for my actions for the rest of my life. I was OK with that, I deserved to, I was a piece of shit for what I had done, and I deserved everything I got from it.

My parents felt differently. We argued for about two weeks, I didn't want my father's help, but he kept insisting on getting his friend, Larry Usher, to be my lawyer. He represented the former governor's family, for Christ's sake, and he was good, real good. He was the kind of guy who needed to wear his success on his suit. If they gave honorary badges or medals to lawyers like they did to generals, this guy would have wore everyone one, probably even to bed. Though, as you know, this doesn't happen. Instead he wore two thousand dollar suits, and he really stood out in Indiana. I didn't want to fight this thing in court at all, I wanted it to be a one-day event, they ask me if I'm guilty, I say yes, they sue me, I pay for as long as it takes. The only thing I didn't want was to go to jail, even though I knew I probably deserved to. My father got me when he started talking about how much time Larry said I could get. I just didn't get it, I was no good, my father and mother had raised an average child at best, a really bad child at worst. I had done something despicable but still they wanted me to get off scot-free, as if nothing happened. I saw how blind parents were in this moment, a mother could birth a serial killer and still she would think the world of him. Maybe this was the reason for my downfall; maybe this was the reason for America's downfall. Maybe if I had gone to military school or a boys' school, somewhere neutral, maybe if I started out with nothing and was forced to work my way up. Maybe I would have had drive, or maybe I'm just making excuses. The sad part of this was that the kid's father was a truck driver; they didn't have as much money as we did to buy a fancy lawyer, my parents spent close to fifty grand on Larry Usher, and they never blinked an eye. I cried in my room every day after the court sessions (that mean's I'm gay, right?). The lawyer that they had couldn't compete, he was young, he looked my age, and you could tell he just wasn't confident about speaking in front of a crowd, made me wonder why he chose this profession. The answer was obvious, everyone either becomes a doctor or a lawyer for one reason: the money. This guy was definitely counting the pennies after this gig to remind him why he was standing in front of a crowd, sweating all day. I could tell by the looks of this kid's father and mother that whatever money they were spending was too much, and that if they didn't win, this would financially hurt them for a long time. I mostly kept my head down, and I didn't look at anyone during the whole thing, I was too ashamed. I stopped my pity party after washing my hands in the limestone bathroom that the taxpayers no doubt paid for.

Larry came out of the stall and put his hands on my shoulders. "Hey, that look you're giving in the courtroom, with your head down like that, beautiful. I can see everyone really believes you feel bad for what you did, they're gonna let you off, don't worry about that." He left without washing his despicable hands.

Larry got me out of being questioned by the opposing attorney by having some bogus doctor determine I was mentally unstable. I determined Larry did this because I stated my voice on rightfully being punished for all this. I sat in my seat, wanting to crush the world for what Larry was doing. It was highway robbery on this poor trucking family. I was despicable every second I didn't do anything and then suddenly, just like when I was holding the vodka bottle at that party nights ago, I stood up in the middle of the courtroom. Everyone was looking at me except for Larry rattling on about my so-called drinking problem. How cliché could he be? I wasn't drunk that night. Larry finally turned around when he lost the jury's attention. I stood there for a moment as my hands fell to the table.

The judge, an older woman perplexed by the situation, merely put her hand to her face and looked at me. "Can we help you, Mr. Wright?" she asked, as if this court case had nothing to do with me.

"Yes, you can." I looked at the judge. "Are you truly buying his brand?" You could hear a needle drop as I pointed to Larry.

"Mr. Wright?" the judge calmly spoke, shocked, as if Larry's spouting off about my clean criminal record and good grades actually made her believe that I should be given a second chance.

Larry instantly got a worried look and finally rattled something off. "I think it's obvious here that he's going through a rough period right now, any statement by--"

I quickly cut him off as he motioned for me to sit down. "You know what they should do with you, Larry? They should make a poster of you in front of the American flag, it should read 'The American dream,' because your what's it's all about. Everything this man says is a lie! All he cares about is winning. News flash, Larry! This isn't ESPN! This isn't a basketball game! This is this kid's life!" I then pointed to the judge very sternly. "If you let this guy win and this poor kid has to live without any restitution, you will all have to live with it for the rest of your lives!" I smoothly walked out.

My parents were shocked, everyone was. I walked out of the courthouse, not uttering another word, and no one stopped me. I cried all the way home. I sat in my room, staring at the wall, trying not to cry so that Markus couldn't hear me if he was home.

About two hours later I got a call. It was Larry. "You're a genius!"

"What?"

"You need counseling from a psychologist twice a week, you'll have to pay for the surgeries, but that stunt you pulled in there was what put the nail in the coffin, you're a genius!" Larry and the opposing lawyer had a meeting in the judge's chambers, apparently it was the opposing lawyer who thought that they had lost after what I said, that it was true, I needed help, and that because of the drinking I couldn't be held totally accountable for what I had done. They made a deal. It was apparent that I stood a better chance of losing like I had intended if I hadn't stood up in the middle of the room and pronounced myself guilty. If you do that, then you must be innocent, according to the American judicial system. This is the system at its best. I lived in a very good area, too. It's Indiana, I can't remember the last time I locked my house or my car. It made me wonder how the judicial system worked in the projects of New York, or the deadliest city in the country, whichever city it is this year. There must be serial killers pronouncing themselves guilty all the time just so they can get home quickly to watch the game before they go out for another annual knifing.

I took another week off from work, claiming that there were more court trials, even though there weren't. I was becoming more and more destructive and I couldn't help myself from throwing the lamp I had made in high school shop into my thirty-two-inch flat screen. Fuck television and the lies it told me just so I would buy whatever it was selling. It wasn't worth it, America was the land of the blind and I was one of them, I just couldn't put it all together yet. I just wanted to destroy everything, it wasn't fair, it wasn't right, and I was going to do something about it even if it took me forever.

Me and Markus were playing football in the house; a pleasure both of our parents denied us when we were kids. We would throw it around from hallway to hallway, not in a competitive way, just in a way of boredom from being locked in our cluttered rooms so much. There was this attic in the hallway we couldn't ever seem to get open in our four years of living there. We legitimately tried maybe four times in our whole time living there. We eventually just stopped caring. There was a latch that had rusted over, we couldn't get it to break, we didn't try much because we needed a ladder to get up there, we were both scared of the fall and the shaky ladder we had to use. We were talking about Veronica as we tossed the ball; she had been calling me recently, leaving voice mails for me to call her as I ignored her rings. Markus was stating that I had known her too long to do her that way, and maybe I had her all wrong. Call it the stench in the air, but I felt that Markus wasn't being honest about why I should give her another chance.

"Why?" I asked. "It's over."

What irked me was that he couldn't fully voice his opinion on why he thought I should give her another chance. That I knew her for a long time just wasn't good enough. To be fully honest, I was smoking weed again, so I was paranoid a lot, and Markus didn't know. I didn't want him to, either, because he knew the problems I had with it.

I had been pacing my room the previous nights, the broken television playing fuzz, convinced that people were watching me from outside my covered windows. The things that went through my head then might as well have been cures for cancer as I paced, they were profound on me then, but when I woke up in the morning, they were just forgotten dreams of paranoia. This definitely had an effect on me, as me and Markus were talking, throwing the football around. I asked him why he wanted me to talk to her so badly, I was no doubt ready for confrontation, he could tell it in my voice, I felt. I didn't care, his timidness made me want to know even more. We were in a heated discussion; I would question him deeper and deeper on why he cared whether or not I talked to Veronica. In my mind, he wanted her back in the house so he could get another chance with her. I asked him if that was the reason and whaled the ball at him.

Markus caught it and threw it back harder. "God, you hate everybody right now, don't you?" he asked. I threw it back just as hard.

"Nope, just you."

Markus caught it. I didn't actually think that me saying that would have an effect on Markus like it did. Apparently, he took it to heart and threw it so hard I think he forgot to aim. The look on his face caused me to duck as I thought the ball would take my head off. I didn't hear the ball hit anything, so I stood up, looking for it. The ball then hit the attic door, causing the ball and the door to fall from the ceiling. Me and Markus both looked at each other, then we looked up through the opening of the attic. Markus got a chair from the kitchen, and before we knew it we had beaten our timidness of heights, climbing up into the attic.

Now, what we found is what would ultimately change our lives forever. The blast of it is, I miss the hard days, but that's how it goes, you know? You never really appreciate all the time you have on this silly little planet. The truth of it is, is that you should, all of it, even the bad times, because those are the times right before the good ones, the good ones fly past you so quick, you don't even remember 'em.

The attic didn't look like anything from a scary movie like most might be used to; it pretty much looked like a storage place for an old woman. It was disorganized and cluttered with interesting little artifacts from decades ago. My guess was the forties, but I always get the forties and sixties mixed up. There were old pictures of family, cousins and uncles so distant that there probably wasn't anything else to do with them but store them. I wasn't a big fan of baseball, maybe that's why Markus thought the world of an autographed baseball he found, of some loser named Lou Gehrig, and I didn't. What I found that day was worth more than pennies could buy. It was the kind of day that tells you something dangerous is about to happen. Not in the way of a killer looming around the corner, it was something more serendipitous. It was one of those moments where internally I felt I had to put my ear to the wooden, dusty attic floor, so that I could hear the wind play, as the nostalgia of finding something new in a place that was so old to us.

When I put my ear to the ground and listened, I looked under the antique bed at the same time towards the end of the attic. Under it was this little rusty box with a lock on it. No one had been in this attic for decades. It didn't take too long for the lock to be broken as me and Markus traded off pulling it apart, it was that old. Inside the box was what looked like a diary, although this diary had no hard cover, and the paper was unlike any I had ever seen. It was old, very old.

I was cautious of touching it at first but when I did take hold of it, it was fine. At glance the writing was not of any normal pen, it seemed to be of a quill pen. It was dated very dated, it was hard to read and was stained, not of any accident but stained from time passing, and plenty of years had done damage to this pamphlet.

Markus's interest grew for a bit as we looked at it, but then I noticed when I turned around that he was gone, looking at other things in the attic. My interest remained. For some reason, I never really took it to heart that it was possible for other human beings to have lived on the same block or the same residence, or even the same land as me, or a hundred or even three hundred years ago. It never really seemed real until I touched this paper. Someone had lived and wrote on this piece of paper, struggled as I did with life, then died, leaving this paper behind. I kept thinking about it as I opened and looked through the pages of eloquent handwriting. Thoughts whipped through my head, as I looked at the stained paper, wondering whom this person had been. I read it from that evening, till morning, almost missing work. I couldn't believe it.

At first reading, the pages were somewhat hard to understand, as the person didn't use words I was familiar with. His name was Oliver Earl, which was the name his white owner suggested to his black mother. His first name was the suggested part; his last name was mandatory as it was the owner's last name. It was Oliver's memoirs, unpublished and in first account on this paper.

He wrote about living with his mother and owner in a secluded part of Georgia. Oliver wrote that until age ten he never really realized he was a slave until he called Mr. Earl, his owner, Father. Mr. Earl was white and denied Oliver as his kin. Oliver's mother Anne Earl, told Oliver in confidence after Oliver got old enough to be suspicious. Before then, Oliver never saw his mother get a lashing before, and never saw his mother cry. Oliver's mother Anne, Mr. Earl and his real father had a complicated relationship. There were no other slaves on the grounds, Mr. Earl raised the chickens and goats along with the garden and occasionally had Oliver help.

Most of Oliver's time was spent playing and swimming with Belle, the daughter of Mr. Earl and Oliver's half-sister. The daughter didn't live with them, and neither did the mother, they were both white and were separated from Mr. Earl. I assumed divorce wasn't looked upon gracefully in those days, which was my estimation on why Mr. Earl still told outsiders he was married to Belle's mother. This couldn't have been more false though, and in fact in Oliver's memoirs, Oliver's Mother Anne and Mr. Earl slept in the same room most nights.

Later, when Oliver was older, Anne confessed that the reason he bought her was very odd to her. When she was first bought he told her that he didn't need her to do housework or yard work that badly, but told her it would be nice if she did housework when it was needed. He also talked to her and told her he was lonely but didn't expect her to fulfill his needs physically unless she wanted to. The two got to know each other over the months on this secluded farm and eventually, Anne fell in love with her owner, and a little while after, Oliver was born. Since the beginning of finding out that Anne was pregnant, Mr. Earl always told her that no one could ever know that Oliver was his. Oliver wrote that some people did know though, Belles mother for one. Mr. Earl was probably fifty or sixty, and Oliver's mother was around sixteen when they had Oliver. Mr. Earl was wealthy due to his family name; the reason for this wealth was unknown. They lived quite well though, and slavery never really entered Oliver's mind until the moment he called Mr. Earl father, and later on Sundays when they would head into town for church. Slaves were bought on Sunday oddly enough.

It was at the age of fifteen for Oliver, when his father and his mother's relationship began to waver. Anne had stopped sleeping with Mr. Earl in the same room, and started sleeping with Oliver, most nights she would cry herself to sleep. Oliver would try to console her but Anne seemed to favor crying alone. Mr. Earl began seeing Belle's mother again after church on Sundays. Belle told Oliver of this and for the first time they talked about the possibility of being kin. Belle wasn't convinced as she said she had seen mixed slaves before and they were always lighter in skin. Oliver however knew the truth and cared not to talk much of it. Oliver knew that Belle had grown to liking Oliver, and probably just hoped that deep down her first kiss wasn't from her half brother slave.

After reading that they had kissed, I was curious if they had done other things, if they had, Oliver kept it secret from his writing, just as he had to do when writing. It was illegal then to teach a slave how to read or write. Mr. Earl taught him when he was a small child, he never had much of a problem in being caught except once when he was younger and read things aloud in front of the townsfolk not knowing any better. Mr. Earl later told Oliver about it when he was older, Mr. Earl would sit on the porch and laugh about it as he told Oliver, he would tell Oliver that they were lucky he had no enemies around town who wanted to feel burdened enough to rat Mr. Earl out.

As Mr. Earl and Anne's relationship grew more tiring on both of them, so did the Civil War. The war seemed like it was in a different country to Oliver though. Oliver's mother Anne began to tell Oliver that she thought Mr. Earl was planning his escape from them, and that if the south didn't win, and the slaves weren't free, that no doubt Mr. Earl would let them go. I was shocked to read that Oliver and his mother actually prayed for the south to win. They had a good life with Mr. Earl though, and to their account, the north winning would break up their family. Oliver found it hard to believe that Mr. Earl would say goodbye to his mother so easily if the north won.

Anne started being harsher with Oliver about doing chores, and said that he needed to realize what it was like out there. This scared Oliver as Oliver was at the age where he could be counted on to do very hard work, and wasn't considered a boy. Every time Oliver didn't do a chore to Anne's liking, Anne would tell Oliver that it was better that he learned now rather then later. Anne scared Oliver with stories of punishment from the slave fields she worked on when she was younger. Oliver wanted to confront Mr. Earl about this but Mr. Earl spent less and less time with Oliver. It seemed that their relationship had suffered due to the suffering of the relationship between Mr. Earl and Anne.

Oliver laid it out as if it had happened to him yesterday. Mr. Earl was on his way back from staying yet another night in town with Belle's mother. Oliver saw him coming down the dirt path to their secluded farm just as he did many mornings. Mr. Earl's first home was in town with Belle's mother, he had a lot more history with Belle's mother than he did with Oliver's. After their falling out, he bought the farm that he lived with Anne and Oliver on.

Mr. Earl came down the path commonly as he always did and without any emotion on his face at all. Mr. Earl brought Oliver and Anne out on the porch and told them that the war was over, and that they were free to go where they chose. Mr. Earl walked into the house after leaving Oliver and Anne to believe they were not to enter except for collecting some of their few items. Oliver didn't want to go anywhere and neither did Anne, although at the time, it seemed like she played more like a bitter girlfriend then a free slave.

Oliver wrote that she collected her things and some other things that weren't hers in a fierce manner that scared Oliver, but was in no doubt aimed for Mr. Earls view. Mr. Earl carried on as if he had not a feeling in the world for them, and treated them more as lost property than a lost family. Oliver always felt, even though Mr. Earl denied it out in the open, that the way Mr. Earl touched Oliver and the way he spoke with Oliver, was all the confession Oliver ever needed.

From there, Oliver and his Mother Anne lived no more luxuriously as they once did. Ironically Oliver and his mother Anne felt more like slaves being free, as citizens of society, than they did as Slaves. Oliver's mother told him that she had forgotten what it was like to be a slave, and that she felt more like a slave being free than she ever did living with Mr. Earl. She had convinced herself that she was free living with Mr. Earl, and that it would always be that way.

Oliver worked cutting down timber for the rest of his life, and took care of his mother. Oliver's boss cutting timber treated him more like a slave then when he actually was a slave. Oliver didn't feel free because he had no choice but to work and cut timber, so that he could provide for himself and his mother. The only freedom Oliver wrote of was the choice to quit and sell his labor to another man, but he didn't because he knew that it would be just as hard, and just as unfulfilling.

Reading Oliver's memoirs was remarkable, and I recommend picking it up, but well, we'll get into that later. It was after reading his memoirs and returning to work that morning, standing behind the counter, waiting for someone to tell me what to do, that I realized what I was. I realized my problem with life. I spent a majority of my time, my precious time I will never get back on this planet, as did Oliver, doing something I didn't want to do. The connection between me and Oliver as I soon realized, didn't stop there. It was between Oliver and Markus, Oliver and our boss, and Oliver with everyone working behind a counter making just enough to survive.

The point was that I never felt better than the days I called into work sick. I slept, I read, I watched interesting movies that made me think. I won the super bowl with the colts on my X-Box. Then when the day came toward its end, a dread loomed, I knew that I would be forced to do something I didn't want to do, just to ensure I could have food and shelter, something we all as human beings should be entitled to. Everyone I knew was like Oliver, we were slaves and didn't know it. Without working at one of these shitty dead end jobs of existence, we would all be homeless and hungry. I knew that my shitty job roughly made millions of dollars per store worldwide. Meanwhile I barely had eight hundred dollars in my account at any given time. I was surviving at best.

I realized then, that slavery never ended, they just decided to call it minimum wage. The wealthy upper-class in a capitalist system is very small, they rely on the poor which is people like me, to do their work on their owned land, providing them the majority of the wealth, while giving the working class nearly none of it. They are also taking something more important than that, our time. No human being's life is worth eight dollars an hour, how would anyone ever figure it would be? Each moment that passes, is a moment in time we will never get back, ever.

It was the illusion that in America now, we are born free. That's a lie, and Oliver's memoirs made me realize that. The truth is that we are free to sell our labor to whomever we want, that's where the freedom ends. The little money that we acquire will be spent on shelter, food, and clothing. The same was given to slaves for their labor, only now we have the illusion of choice, between what kind of clothes, food, and shelter we have. When I thought about the years I wasted standing behind the counter, it made me sick. I wish I could take it back, I wanted to quit right there, but I couldn't. If I did I'd have to find another job and nothing's scarier then wondering if you're going to make rent.

It was obvious to me, then and there, that in fact I wasn't free. In reality I had very little freedom to do anything. I had no money, I was obligated to be at my job when they wanted me to be, and if I didn't comply, I would be fired, without food, shelter or clothing. I remembered being taught in the third grade how we lived in the best country in the world because we were free. That was a lie that I had always believed.

The worst part of it is that there doesn't seem to be a way out. The obedient working class would somehow have to wake up, just as I did, ban together and put an end to this unfair spool of lies. I might as well keep dreaming of Taryn Manning from "Hustle And Flow" in a thong, laying on my stained rug. Then I realized, if somehow I could get Oliver's memoirs to the public maybe that could change things. Maybe people would come to the realization just as I did following the reading. I smiled for the first time in a long time as I stood behind that counter. There were pregnant skanks all around looking for clothes, diapers and toys, all for their newborns. I needed to do this for them I thought, so that this new generation won't be standing where I am. Wow, I finally have it, I said to myself. I took off my stupid blue vest, and ran out the door.

I began using Markus's Hollywood Creative Directory, and I began sending emails to publishing companies that day. Markus became intrigued; finally after a lot of talking to him about what I had read, he read it too. At a much slower pace than I had read it, Markus read it, and he got what I was saying at least and agreed. Markus had a different opinion though; he wasn't totally convinced anyone would pick it up to make it into a book. We got into a bit of an argument about it.

We went to Barnes and Nobles to finish the debate; he started showing me what he was talking about. He was grabbing books off the shelves to show me examples.

"Look there are no vampires, there are no soldiers blasting the shit out of terrorists. These memoirs are just this black dude and his family, the only stories published or made into movies these days are about super heroes or Hobbits," Markus said.

"Ah ha!" I said, as I picked up a book with Barack Obama's face on it. "He's black, it's popular to be black now."

Markus looked at me with doubt.

"Yes but because of Barack Obama, racism is over. No one is going to be knocking down our door to publish a book that was written two zillion years ago."

He had a point; this was the age of the stupid I thought. Obviously things needed to change, and if anything could cause things to change, it was Oliver's memoirs. So I copied over every page, word for word to my computer and made a PDF file of it ready to go out.

Markus suggested that I should copyright it just in case he was wrong. I did with the hopes that he was. I copyrighted it online as Markus huddled behind me watching with a smirk. I was just about to put it in my name, when he said that I should put it in his name too.

"Why?" I asked.

"I helped find it too, if it wasn't for me throwing that football neither of us would of found it," Markus stated.

"Sure, I guess your right," I said. I didn't care who had the copyright; I just wanted people to read this.

We bet fifty bucks on if the book would be published within the first month, and then we bet twenty bucks the next month. When the third month came around I realized it was too hard to even get anyone to read it. There were several companies that told me that they only read material from established writers' recommendations. So unless Oliver forgot to mention in his memoirs he was long standing friends with Tom Clancy, this looked to be way harder than I thought it was going to be.

Somehow in the minds of these publishing companies, the only talented writers were friends of already established writers,..........RIGHT. Aside from the hundreds of places that didn't take it the few that would take the material said it wasn't for them, or that it wasn't marketable enough, or blah after blah, blah, blah. Markus was right, they all wanted Lord Of The Ring rip offs.

It was all about money. This world, this country, had become all about money, and why you ask? These wealthy publishing companies didn't want to end up like me, working behind a counter, they didn't want to lose their comfy jobs and become slaves. The book that maybe could have an impact, and open peoples minds so that possibly, maybe someday, people wouldn't ever have to worry about working for some asshole who wanted to get rich off of their labor for millions of dollars while he gives his workers the lint from his pockets, wasn't marketable. Americana at its finest.

I also found that one of the companies thought that the material wasn't appropriate. Where's the freedom of speech? What happened to that? Well we have that as long as nobodies are talking amongst our selves. If we want to start doing important things with that liberty, like getting our voices out to millions of people, there are big shots with grey hair and old views ready to shoot those missiles out of the sky. After all, they have millions of dollars to protect. They depend on poor people to get them their breakfast, lunch, and dinner.

The funny thing I kept wondering was what are all these billionaires going to do with their money when they are in a casket? Do they bury the money with them, inside the casket? After all, they did work their entire lives for pieces of paper with dead presidents on them, they might as well try and take it with them if they can, hopefully it will help them with where they are going.

I started thinking about all the people out there that could probably change the world, but would never get to because they didn't have a credit card big enough. Plain and simple, it doesn't feel right. I as well as everyone else didn't ask to be given life, no one asks for any of this, and unless you can ensure a fantastic life for the child you give life to, you shouldn't be creating life freely.

It's selfish, all that Angelina Jolie, save the children bullshit. (She just cares about how famous she can get with it anyway.) If millions of children weren't born in starving countries, we wouldn't have this problem. All children are not innocent little saints though; they are assholes in waiting like everyone else. Yes, we were all cute once, but all adults have had moments of being assholes to someone, if they're not assholes every moment of their lives anyway. Just as these money hungry rich people were once innocent little children, they are now the assholes that won't publish Oliver's memoirs because they don't want to lose any of their precious paper.

I started resenting my parents, what gave them the audacity to give me life, or to give anyone life? Why would anyone think that they had enough of the world's answers to have a child? I was standing in my room pacing back and forth, but the room wasn't big enough anymore, I needed to escape but couldn't, even though I could walk right out the door. Where would I go? The only thing anyone can do in this world is spend money, and at the moment I had zero.

I never went back to work or even called to explain myself. They probably didn't even realize I was gone. They remembered to stop writing the checks though. I had wasted three months of my life trying to do something good for once and got nowhere. The world didn't want anything good though it just wanted money. I was "borrowing" money from my parents, I say, "borrowing" because it was my parents and they weren't gonna ask for it back. They were paying my rent and even though I liked the three-month break from slavery, I hated that my parents were paying for it, I hated burdening them, and they had their own problems.

I started hanging out more at my parent's house on weekends. The loneliness would kill me sometimes. Veronica was starting to get to me too, I wanted to talk to her, I wanted her around, I missed her touch, and I missed having her in my bed at night just to hold. Of course I didn't want to admit it, not even to myself, let alone her.

I was lingering in my parent's kitchen around six PM after waking up at about five PM. I spent the day sleeping after watching HBO all night, I was silently wishing I could get out of this mess I never asked for. My father lingered in the kitchen after work in one of those ways that made me think that he's not really in the kitchen to eat, even though he pretended to look through the refrigerator. He asked in an upbeat manner,

"How's it going?"

My lip curled as I felt his subtle way of trying to see when I was going to be able to start working again.

"I'm gonna get my job back, there's no reason to beat around the bush," I replied back.

"Oh," he said. "Well, me and your mother were talking about Nanny."

"Nanny?" I asked.

Nanny was my mother's grandmother, to tell you in short, she was a fugitive most of her life for throwing a woman out a store window for looking at her husband in the wrong way. When I think about it now there were a lot of similarities between us, I wasn't buying it then though. Nanny lived to a ripe old age of ninety; she defied health experts of today by eating a pack of greasy bacon and fat drenched gravy every day. My mother had fond memories of Nanny burning the furniture on the back lawn when she thought that grandpa had slept with her sister. The truth was that my great Grandpa had gone shopping with Nanny's sister to buy Nanny a purse for her birthday. Years later Nanny still believed that Grandpa had been cheating on her with her sister.

The only memories I had of nanny were when we went to visit. My mother would bring her purse up to the attic so that Nanny wouldn't rifle through it. I also remember my mother telling me when and when not to speak at night in the attic, Nanny would listen up against the door to see if we were talking about her.

"What about Nanny I asked?"

"Well," my father said, "Maybe you should see somebody?"

"See somebody?" I asked.

"Someone you could talk to," he replied.

I hated the typical cliché of people who couldn't admit something was wrong with them and would refuse to see a psychologist. Maybe I did need one I thought, even though I resented the subtle comparison to Nanny at the time. I kind of felt like maybe it was just who I was and that I couldn't change that, and I was about to find out.

Before I could say yes, he said that if I did, he wouldn't make me work any more, and that I could continue to try and peddle around the book I found. I suddenly and quickly stopped caring about the burden I was putting on my parents and thought that them paying for my way as I went and talked to someone for "help" was probably fair enough as it was their arrogance that decided it would be a good idea to give me life.

The person I usually talked to was Veronica; I missed what I had with her even though the part that we shared with each other was just one side of the two-way mirror. That's how all relationships are though, she couldn't tell me that she desired to sleep with Markus, and I couldn't tell her that I desired the skank who sold us foot longs at Subway.

I started seeing Mrs. Bell once a week at her over embellished office in Indianapolis. She thought she was more elegant than she really was, as if that degree she had from some wanna be Ivy league school that I had never heard of made her better than me. She was probably fifty; she had her grey frizzy hair in a bun and tended to wear clothes that really weren't her age, like skinny jeans.

From first glance she seemed to have more problems than me. That's the hypocrisy of seeing a professional, no one is perfect, but yet there are people who get paid to tell you what's wrong with you. It seemed right off that she was trying to classify me in some genre of over critical analysis. If it were up to me I would classify Mrs. Bell under whatever would be symptoms of needing to prove your intellect and success by buying an expensive modern interior designer. She had all the typical decorations that would be classified as modern, but in five years she would have to redecorate to stay up with the "times."

It started to baffle me that I was suppose to take this woman seriously, her approach didn't seem to be from someone who spent their entire lives studying the mind, but of someone who watched Lorraine Bracco's character too closely the night before during the marathon of the Sopranos.

The first few weeks were pretty lame, and then we started talking about Veronica. Veronica had stopped trying to get me to call her back. The thing was that I secretly knew I was being too hard on Veronica, and that there was absolutely nothing to suggest that Veronica had cheated on me or that she even wanted to. I was over thinking things and coming to these conclusions by myself. OK so maybe the psychiatrist helped a little bit. Maybe the people with the most problems are the ones who are capable of helping people the most. Either way, if it was just the gap in my bed at night that needed to be filled, or the somewhat valid things I started to realize with Mrs. Bell, I was prepared to give Veronica a call, and actually speak with her instead of not saying a word like the last time she called. Would life really be too boring if we all just got along? Probably, but at this point I just wanted to feel her love again. This part was the deciding factor. I have had sex with people and felt nothing or awkwardness, that was common, but when me and Veronica had sex, I felt it, I felt every inch of love she had for me, and I'm sure she felt what I had for her. It wasn't just during intercourse either; it was when we touched each other, or when she had her mouth down below. That was the best part; I had never had a girl perform oral sex on me like Veronica. I have had girls tell me that I have a big penis, maybe its something they just tell everyone, but I hadn't ever seen a girl that could put every inch of my penis down their throat. I couldn't fathom ever having anything that large down my throat like that without barfing all over the place.

She did it because she loved me, I could tell by the way she did it, pounding my thing down her mouth like that was no easy task. Words are just that from a girl, words, you can't really trust that what they are saying is true, but if you can get one to give you oral like this, then you can trust that when they say they love you they mean it.

I called her after thinking of how awkward it would be between us, looking at myself in the reflection of my own mirror. I didn't want to look at myself, I felt like something on my face was telling me that I was right to begin with, I didn't listen.

She answered as if she didn't know who it was. This is the age of Caller ID, I knew that this wasn't true, and that she wanted to seem as if she was unaware I existed anymore. To my surprise she told me things I never would have expected. She told me that she missed me, and I hadn't said anything yet. She told me that she was sorry and that it was her fault that everything happened and that she loved me, and hopes that we can work everything out. I was very surprised and speechless as I hadn't planned to say anything, but was prepared to apologize if I needed to. This worked out much better.

She came over and suddenly we fell back into things, only this time, things were really, really good between us. We were having sex two, sometimes three times a day, and all was more then I could ask for. I told her about the deal I had struck with my father, and about Oliver's book. She skimmed through it and seemed impressed with my new passion, she could tell it meant a lot to me that I get Oliver's book out there. Talking to someone like Veronica about it, someone I trusted, really made me see that I had more passion than I even knew. I told her about my new discoveries after reading the book, about how our freedoms were really just an illusion.

I think maybe I was too passionate about it over the following weeks, so much so that I decided to stop talking to her about it at times. And maybe this was just my paranoia, but it seemed that Veronica's facial expressions started hinting at some jealousy. Suddenly, after about two weeks of this, I found myself asking for sex again, having to masturbate again. Her shrewdness came back as well, along with that face that was constantly frustrated when I was around.

Veronica had just gotten her wisdom teeth out and we were planning to go out and see our friends from high school who attended IU University for St. Patrick's Day. We were in my room and Veronica was in pretty bad pain, she was stretched out on my bed. We hadn't done it for awhile, so I tried my luck by kissing her stomach, one of her hot spots, but she quickly turned me away as she didn't want to be bounced around. Markus had barged into my room twice touring Tory Lane's new video on some website. Veronica wasn't a fan of porn, big surprise as most women aren't. In my opinion it's jealousy, truthfully I think all women want to be the center of every man's world, and when there is a gangbang going on with one girl in the center of eight cocks, women everywhere are twitching their eyelids with anger and rage.

Veronica had been good with being invested in our relationship recently, holding my hand or arm when we would go out together, really being invested in me for a change. I actually began to have a new trust for her and was suddenly; in the manliest way possible, wondering what it would be like if we were married. I know, I'm a big pussy right? I thought about kids suddenly, and what it would be like to have a daughter or a son with her.

Deep down though, I wasn't ever impressed with the word love, what does it mean anyway? By definition from the dictionary, I hadn't seen it in my lifetime ever, not from my parents, not from neighbors, not from anybody. When you think about it, it's impossible for anyone to satisfy someone's needs completely. I knew this but still I said it to Veronica, I mean I care about Veronica, and what other words in the English dictionary can you use to express to someone you care about. I guess you can always escape to the princess diaries if you have to. That's the only place I can think of where love really exists, books, movies, and of course music. The music industry has seemed to forget that there are other human conditions out there worth singing about. That's the tragedy of life I suppose, that everything changes, and nothing lasts. That's what everyone forgets, that's what I forgot, that as human beings, we are changing constantly, Veronica was changing, I was changing. My hope that she would stay the way I wanted her would never come true.

I had left the house to get me and Veronica something to eat, it was Burger King I think, nothing special, but I felt bad for her and would have gotten her anything since she was in so much pain. I got her the milk shake she wanted and went into my room expecting to find her asleep on my comforter. She wasn't to be found, wondering where she was suddenly I heard laughter, it was coming from Markus's room, and sure enough, Veronica who was in too much pain to get her own food, was suddenly feeling fine enough to be laughing at every fucking word Markus said inside his room.

It wasn't the kind of laughter that you see a normal person do when they are genuinely laughing at something. It was the kind of laughter that says, "I like you, look at me laugh at everything you say. Now fuck me."

I was pissed. I dropped her milk shake on the floor and went into my room, they didn't know I was back, but they knew it then. I was so fed up with her, everything was slowly going back to the way things were, I knew that if I brought her to this party in Bloomington, that she would be back playing the same games.

Veronica and Markus came into my room. Veronica was doing a good job at trying to make me think she had no idea what she was doing. Markus was a bit timid and probably knew what had irked me. I could have blamed Markus too, but I just blamed Veronica. I realized that I was trying to make Veronica be someone that she would never be. She would always be the same flirtatious girl who likes to play games with the guy she's with, and I would always be the guy who hated it. I shook it off in front of them; I told them that I had just seen a stray dog get hit by a semi. They knew I had a love for animals, and even though what I told them was a lie, at the end of the night, I felt it was true.

We traveled down to Bloomington together in separate cars. Veronica went with me, but I didn't talk much, she gave up trying to get me to talk and we listened to shitty music on the radio that I drowned out with my thoughts. It was a two-hour drive so I did a lot of thinking about our supposed love for each other. It wasn't love I thought, it was just two human beings scared of being alone, just like it was for everyone else. Two human beings that didn't want to take the plunge into life.

She wanted to fuck Markus, but she didn't. She didn't because I was holding her back. By fucking him, I would find out, dump her, and she would be alone. People are so scared to be alone that they will deny themselves what they want in the moment. A moment that I might remind you will never come back again. It goes through all of our heads before we don't do something like this.

She was thinking, "What if I don't find anybody else?"

And all Markus was probably thinking was, "Who would be the one not to move out of this exceptionally cheap place we have?"

Markus and Veronica didn't really care about me as a person, they cared about me as an object, and how the object would affect their every day lives if they screwed. I believe that's how most people are though. Usually they give some other excuse for their actions, like how much they care for the other person. I was beginning to think no one cared about anyone in this world. I was probably right. I was thinking about all of this on the trip down to Bloomington when suddenly I heard the screams of Veronica in the passenger seat.

"What?" I said.

Veronica replied, "I said I love you, you didn't say it back."

This was something she would do when she knew I was mad at her, she would say, "I love you" just to see how mad I was by the way I replied. I replied genuinely wondering about this question.

"Do you really think you love me?" She replied with a look of confusion.

"What's wrong with you? Of course I love you."

I didn't want to get into it with her, it would be just another denial that I was supposed to take as truth, and If I didn't take it as truth, then the gloves would really come off. If Veronica for some reason told me to believe that she had magic powers, and for some reason, I don't know, maybe because I don't live in Lord of the Rings and magic powers don't exist, and if I didn't believe her, she would flip. The magic thing wasn't the case though, she wanted me to believe that she loved me, I guess when you think about it, it is a form of magic, people just assume it's real and it exists. She pretended to have no idea why I was mad. I was done with this.

I was later standing in the middle of this large room, college kids in togas all around me that I barely knew, all talking to each other and I thought, if she wants to be a whore, I should let her. If she wanted to believe that the way she was treating me was love, then I should prove to her that it wasn't. I figured it would be easier on both of us this way. I began speaking up at this party, only it was toward Markus and Veronica who conveniently were already conversing in the Mardi Gras decorated kitchen.

"Drink up," I said to both of them. Not much of a drinker myself, this surprised both of them as they looked at me like sheep.

"Bahhh," they said.

"Lets get really wasted," I said. I kept pouring it, and they kept drinking it. I was pretending to have a good time and they bought it. It was late and drunken kids started driving their way home. Just the three of us in a nice cozy bed somewhere I thought. If they were going to fuck, I wanted to see it. I wanted proof for my own eyes that Veronica, a girl I had been with since high school, was a no good, dime a dozen slut.

They insisted on leaving but I talked them into a room where they were falling all over the place and slurring their words with dumb laughter. The room looked as if it were decorated by someone's mother, it was obviously a girls room but I knew that the only person in the house was in their bed already, the other roommates were actually on a school trip to Ireland and weren't expected to be back.

Veronica was pretty much passed out on this queen-sized bed. I did a good job at making sure that Veronica was hammered, she was a light drinker. Six shots did her in and she was incomprehensible after the seventh. I woke Veronica up after locking the door and started kissing her. Markus was laying on the other side of the bed and got up, leaving the room as I began to put my hand down Veronica's pants. I stopped and Veronica quickly passed back out. I followed Markus out of the room and asked him where he was going. Markus was keeping himself up by holding on to the hallway with his forearm.

"Finding another room," he slurred.

"It's OK Markus, come back in here," I said.

"You're doing, you're, you're, doing her though," he slurred.

I wasn't about to argue with someone this drunk, so I chauffeured him back into the room where Veronica was passed out. As I did, I told him that there was this girl that really wanted to fuck him. I turned off the lights and told him to take off his pants. Markus stumbled and asked who the girl was. This was the same room he was just in a moment ago, and suddenly, it was foreign to him, or maybe, it was just his way of doing what he really wanted to.

I woke Veronica up pulling on her head. She was like a puppet as I guided her where I wanted her to go. I led her head towards Markus's penis as she was on all fours. As if it was me, she started going to town. We stuffed her like an Oreo cookie for about an hour. I fucked her in the ass and in her pussy, as Markus fucked her in the mouth. They would stumble around drunk like, but never in a million years would I ever believe that they never really knew what they were doing. They knew, they knew exactly what they were doing. Everyone always knows. Liquor is a nice excuse though, but in the end, it just makes you do what you really wanted to.

She moaned like a whore, and I fucked her with little empathy. I made sure to get my fill, as I knew I would want nothing to do with her after this. I was fucking her in the mouth and Markus was fucking her in her pussy when I told him to cum inside her. He was about to cum, and then suddenly he puked all over her. I pulled on her head calling her a slut and bent her over towards me. I felt all the anger and frustration in my life seep out of me and into her in that moment as she moaned in both pain and pleasure. I came in her ass and then once again in her vagina as Markus was passed out on the bed.

I didn't sleep that night, I stood out on the porch, and I didn't feel anything. Things were clear in my head, I could breathe and just be for a little bit. Like an animal with a brain so small it was unable to think of anything but survival. I wish things could of stayed that way. In reality it's the only thing that matters, modern society has made survival too simple, and so simple that we have to resort to fighting amongst each other about trivial things.

The ride home was quiet to say the least; I could tell Veronica's hangover must have been immense. Not immense enough to have not known what had happened. A typical thing that all women say when they go out drinking and regret what they did. Which is exactly what happened. We had gotten back to my place without a thing being said. She came in to get her coat that she had left and started acting like things were normal. I wasn't too surprised. I pretended like she wasn't there, but when she sat down, that's when I asked her to leave.

She asked me what was wrong and I asked her if she was serious. She then said, with the tone of voice she uses when she's lying,

"What happened last night?"

Something came over me so intense that I screamed.

"You were a whore last night! That's what happened!"

She put her polka dot purse around her shoulder and left. I didn't know it then, but when she left she didn't just walk out quick like, probably because she knew what she had done. She kind of lingered there by my door for maybe five seconds, as if she wanted me to stop her. I looked away as I knew that she was trying reel me in. I soon looked back at her as if I was waiting for to leave, which I was, I really wanted nothing to do with her.

But at some point during those five seconds, maybe in the spur of the moment, maybe in one last ditch effort to try and ruin my life, she did something that would prove to be the best thing that ever happened to me, I'll get more into that later.

Markus didn't come home that night, and I didn't blame him. He came back the next day though, we didn't really communicate for the next few weeks. Depression was on and off surprisingly, I sent out emails and made phone calls, agents wanted nothing to do with Oliver's memoirs, and neither did publishing companies. I kept trying though.

I started spending a lot of time outside. You spend so many days of life in little boxes called rooms and cars; it's no wonder kids take sawed off shotguns and blast up schools. Sometimes I felt like that, just blasting people to get out my anger. People need to kill other people, there is too much control with the way things are.

When the world was at the beginning, and humans hunted instead of shopped, it was natural for humans to kill other humans. Now things were sadly too simple, and in control. Every day of my life had been regulated by someone else. This was the first time I was truly free, I wanted to test my freedom. I wanted to take someone's meaningless life. Someone who thought their life was meaningful. I sat in the middle of the woods and contemplated it for a few seconds, the risk was too great and deep down, I didn't have it in me, I knew it was wrong, I did for a split second believe I could get away with it though. I thought for a split second how I could do it, and get away with it, but the chances of being behind bars, and finding out what waited for me after this life, was far too unsettling to me. In reality, having outside forces determined my decisions in life, made me behind bars already.

Just as when I was going to school or working eight to ten hours when I didn't want to be, I was a slave, sitting in the woods. I realized that society wasn't a good thing. It was slavery, and I was enslaved by people in power, people in power from past and present. By choosing to live in society, and by their rules, I was giving them the power over my limited time on earth.

To tell you the truth, I don't know why I even bothered writing this, the people in power would never publish this, they have too many millions to protect, too great of a chance that people will do the same thing I'm about to. I guess there are stranger things that have happened though; I mean people get abducted by aliens all the time, don't they? So I guess there is always hope right? I wanted to stay hidden in these woods, away from everyone and everything, society made me want things that I didn't need, made me dream things I would never see.

Unfortunately I left the woods and went back to my car and drove home. I had to, I was unable survive in the wilderness; I had became too dependent on other people. I was taught how to shop instead. The depression was seeping back in, and seeping back hard. I wasn't eating, I lost ten pounds and I couldn't sleep, the best I could do was rest my eyes, but I would soon wake up. Sitting around was the worst part of it, the boredom of being alone.

I wanted to do something but I couldn't. To do anything in this world costs money; eating out, renting or going to a movie, what else is there to really do? I'm surprised I'm not charged to breathe. I shouldn't be giving anyone any ideas, though. Existing, being, it's all just way too overrated. When I try to think back to before I was born, all I see is darkness. Darkness isn't all that bad, I didn't have any of the problems I do now. I think that's where all people begin, just darkness. It's peaceful, why would anyone want to disturb that by bringing a human being into the light, into this world?

I was at home, staring at the ceiling, when I decided that Oliver's book would be better off in a safe deposit box instead of sitting in my room. I got up off my ass to get it off the bookshelf, and instead of finding it, I didn't... Yes, that's right, I had suddenly misplaced a two to three hundred year old pile of paper. I didn't freak out... at first. I calmly started looking around and gradually I started freaking out. A better term would be LOSING MY FUCKING MIND! I turned my bedroom upside down, I didn't finish until every useless thing I owned was piled up in the middle of the floor. My bed was turned upside down, I had broken a mirror out of frustration, forget the seven years bad luck, I had just lost fifty years worth of good luck. I gave up on my room, realizing that it wasn't there after about thirty minutes of frustration, and asked Markus. Markus's blank stare let me know that he didn't know. I started looking through the living room, I knew I was wasting my time but I had to do something. I gradually realized that the book wasn't anywhere near my person, or the crack house I called home. I sat down on the couch in the living room as I was sweating with fear of not finding the book; all I could do was rest my head in my hands. Markus came in and sat down across from me, eating pears from a can, as he was curious about what was going on. Me and Markus never talked about that night, but we did begin to get to the point where we could be in the same room. I even made him laugh once instead of just sulk around me. So, we were sitting in the living room together, we were just small talking a bit after I had told him that I couldn't find Oliver's book, and then, all of a sudden, as if things could get any worse, he hit me with it. He said he was moving to Los Angeles. With the circumstances being the way they were, I would have thought that I wouldn't have cared, but I did. He had been saving for a while, but I began to think that his dream of being in porn was something he didn't really want, not enough to move from the great state of Indiana, anyway. Markus was leaving within the month, leaving me behind. I officially would have no one with in a few weeks. I acted like I was neutral about him leaving, as best as possible, but I think he knew I wasn't. I stopped thinking about Oliver's book for a brief second; hopefully it wouldn't pick up and leave from its first destination. I just wanted to be done with all people, it wasn't worth it anymore, I needed to just remain alone. I needed to be in the woods, where it was safe and where there was little room for me to get hurt by the everyday drama of society.

I started thinking about how I could get Markus to stay. I needed him to stay for my sanity, if he didn't then inevitably some much worse roommate would come in with problems that would make Markus look like a saint. I mean, Markus was a good friend, whatever that means, right? When I was alone, at least I wasn't totally alone, and knew that there was another breathing, blooded animal behind a wall close to mine, going through the same problems as I was. As much as I hate to admit it, living in the woods was a pipe dream. I couldn't survive there, not realistically. I wanted to make it work, but it was like trying to make a square block fit in to piece of wood carved into a circle. The best I could do was make the best of things in this moment, and at this moment, I needed Markus to stay. I mean, who else would be able to call the police if I decided to hang myself in the bathroom or something? People need other people so that someone can call the morgue for emergencies like that, otherwise you just end up hanging there and rotting. It was selfish trying to get Markus to stay, I knew that, but I didn't care, I needed to try. I thought and thought, I racked my brain for hours, thinking of a way that would make him stay. I was sitting on the porch; I had recently taken up smoking and was puffing at the first pack I ever bought, American Spirit, the one with the big gaping gay Indian on it. There was a ring on my cell phone, and I looked at the caller ID. It was the most terrifying thing I had ever seen up to that point. Korea, Pakistan, Iraq, and Iran could of all called to tell me that they were bombing Indianapolis Indiana, and that I had about five minutes to live, I still wouldn't have been as scared as I was in this moment. It was Veronica's dad calling. I knew this because I had saved it the one time he had ever called me from his office. It was at the beginning of me and Veronica's relationship, back in high school. We were just sophomores trying to fuck, and Veronica's dad cared a lot more about her than he did now. At least, I thought he didn't care as much about her, I was terrified by the notion of Veronica confessing what had happened that night in Bloomington. Was it possible? Veronica's dad was the kind that would call the police if he thought someone had hurt his daughter. He tried having me arrested once when he caught us naked in her bedroom. This time, he might actually have a case. Veronica and I used to sneak around to have sex back in high school a lot. I wasn't ever aloud in her bedroom so we had to. Veronica would tell her dad that she was going to the high school football game with her friends and that I wasn't going. We'd wait till halftime just in case Veronica's dad had planned on checking up on her. Then Veronica and I would head to the packed parking lot for some unprotected, stupid, crazy sex. Or we would head to the practice field and have sex in the woods. I never knew the score of the football games, but I always kept track of the score between Veronica's father and me - he always lost. Veronica's dad called me when Veronica and I were skipping school; we were having sex in a graveyard. The first cell phone I had due to the thoughts running through my parents' heads of terrorists blowing up the Logansport high school, thanks to nine-eleven, the cell phone companies made bank. My cell phone rang away as I was balls deep in Veronica. Veronica didn't want me to answer it, but I did anyway. All I heard was, "If you know what's good for you, you'll take my daughter back to school, fast." I did, but I made sure to finish off the duty I had begun in that graveyard. It was a big game between Veronica's father and me. He subconsciously wanted to sleep with her, and keep her for himself, an instinct all fathers have that hasn't been evolved out of them yet. If you think about it, it's kind of sick. I mean, why else would an old married man try to keep their daughter from the inevitable, good ol' nasty sex? I wasn't ever really scared of Veronica's father until now. Going to court and explaining what had happened would be horrible.

I answered the phone, this time a little warier than the first.

"Hey, how are you doing?" he asked.

"Uh, fine," I said.

"Look, I know you and Veronica are having problems, but It doesn't mean you and I have to," he said.

I was unsure what to make of this and said, "Um, OK?"

Optimistically he said, "I'd like to meet with you and Markus if that's OK?"

I was worried, I didn't quite know how to get out of this one. "Meet?" I asked.

"Yes, meet," he said.

"Well, what about?" I asked.

"I don't think it's appropriate to speak about it over the phone, meet me tomorrow at noon in my office."

I immediately began thinking of an excuse, a dentist appointment was no good, and Veronica probably told him I wasn't working or going to school anymore. I couldn't think of anything.

"OK?" he asked.

"Um, sure," I said. I figured maybe I could talk him out of killing or arresting me and Markus in person. You know that weight that sunk to the bottom of my stomach right before I whacked that guy with a vodka bottle? That's what happened again. I figured that I wouldn't tell Markus; there was no reason for having both of us killed or arrested. Then I started thinking, would Veronica really tell her dad? How awkward would that be? Then I thought of ways he could have found out. Then it hit me like a shovel to the back of the head. Maybe she was pregnant. That had to be it. She must have told her dad that she was pregnant and when he asked whose it was, Veronica said she didn't know. This was bad; this was very, very fucking bad. I wouldn't be able to get out of this one with my parents' help. I was going to be stuck to the whore for the rest of my life. I was officially dumber than the hillbillies that got the pregnant skanks knocked up at the store.

I didn't sleep at all that night; I paced around my room and hallway, wondering what I should do. I thought that I should tell Markus; then again I thought it would be better for me to take the heat first and then if it happened to be his kid, let him take some heat. After all, I was convinced that he did in fact know what he was doing, even though I was sure that he would claim otherwise. It was a sad predicament for both of us; his trip to L.A. was about to be officially cancelled. It was in fact, partly my fault as well; I had helped him ruin his dreams. I started hoping that the kid was mine, just for his sake. I mean, I had nothing going for me, I decided that I would take responsibility no matter what. I knew Veronica was against abortion, and even though I was against life, I knew that there was nothing I could do to change Veronica's mind. She had been a big advocate for Republicans during all the elections, just because of their stance against abortion. I had even stopped bringing up the subject, it just wasn't worth making her cry, she would get way too emotional about it. I was about to bring someone into the world that was going to hate me for it later.

I was standing in the hall as the sun was rising. I got showered and dressed, sat on my bed, staring at the wall, thinking, until eleven. I couldn't wait any longer so I left and headed for Veronica's house where her dad's office was.

I got there at eleven thirty and waited for about twenty minutes until I couldn't take it any longer and had to go in. Veronica's house is of white pale brick, with well-kept shrubs on the outside. It's a five to seven room house, I can't be quite sure I never counted. I could have always asked the maid who came twice a week or the minimum-wage slaves who came to take care of the lawn.

I rang the doorbell and with in seconds Veronica's dad opened the door. Veronica's dad is named Andrew, he answered the door in dress clothes but without the tie, it seemed like this was going to be atrocious. He had grey hair that was combed over his balding head, but a face that seemed like a little pouty baby. He was smiling when he saw me, which really freaked me out. He brought me in and suddenly his energy and optimistic behavior was starting to catch on. Could this be a trick?

I started to loosen up as he kidded around a bit as we stood in the living room. "The help just got to vacuuming my office, so we'll be in there in a bit."

"What's going on?" I asked as we sat down on the couch.

"We'll get to that in a bit, let's wait until we're in my office," he said.

I was really going crazy thinking about what was going on. I started thinking that maybe since Veronica was pregnant; he wasn't going to take it all that bad and try to kill me. Maybe he had started some kind of yoga treatment that calmed him down and now, instead of yelling at me, he had accepted it. "Is Veronica here?" I asked.

He moved uncomfortably in his chair as if afraid of the question. "Oh, no, sorry about how that all went down, I guess she really wants to focus on going to graduate school."

What the hell is going on? Did Veronica tell him that she broke up with me because she wanted to focus on going to graduate school? I had never heard this from Veronica's mouth. Maybe she was, maybe it would be good for her. This was all too crazy for me, though. I thought I was going to be killed or arrested. So far, Veronica going to graduate school was a way better option.

Veronica's dad took me into his office next. It reeked just like an old successful man's office should, like young pussy. It was a comfy little nook with a Persian carpet. Nice oak desk, some interesting and no doubt expensive duplicates of paintings on the wall. I sat across from him in a comfortable, plush, and leather chair. After a huge relief came to me, I started to wonder and worry more. Well, if she's not pregnant, what the hell am I doing here?

"Oh yeah, where's Markus?" he asked.

"Uh, he couldn't make it, work," I said.

He looked disappointed but then said, "OK, we'll have to talk to him another time then. The reason I brought you here was because of this." He held up Oliver's memoirs.

Suddenly angels began humming and playing harps. I couldn't believe he had it. "Where did you get that?" I asked as I ripped the memoirs from his hands. It wasn't obvious to me then, as the shock of him holding Oliver's memoirs wasn't making me think quite clearly.

He told me with a look of discomfort, "Veronica came home early in the morning one day, it was obvious she was upset about something, so I walked into her room to talk to her about it and I see her just about to light this masterpiece of Oliver's up in flames. This is a part of American history, Richard. I don't know if you're aware of this but I'm an editor for a publisher called - (For legal purposes I'd rather not say). We did some research on this and saw that you and Markus have the copyright to it. That's fine, you found it, from what I hear, and there is no living family of Oliver's today, we checked. So, to prematurely ejaculate the conversation, my publisher would like to make an offer, to both you and Markus."

"An offer?" I said. The thought of being free like Bill Gates quickly entered my mind. "Uhh, how much?" I asked, with dollar signs replacing my pupils.

With his chin pointing down in a sly way, he stated, "Because of its historical significance, we're prepared to offer you a sum that we've never offered to anyone. The offer is two million dollars." Obviously he and his publisher had dollar signs for pupils, too, although no one representing the publisher was present. From what I gathered later, Veronica's dad wanted to meet with me first, before he had me meet with the publisher. He wanted me to secure in writing that he would receive fifteen percent for helping us get the deal, and that he would also receive his normal fee for editing the book. I signed it right away, and all Markus had to do was sign it. It all sounded like gravy to me, I was totally fine with Veronica's dad getting whatever, and I was totally fine sharing with Markus, even though I was secretly skeptical of any real claim he had on the book. The only thing that really mattered to me was that people would be able to finally read the damn thing. I had worked on getting it out to publishers for what seemed to be forever, a long, lonely forever, while Markus bet on how many times I would fail. Now, my success by luck was going to profit for Markus. I soon realized that this was a perfect way to keep Markus around. This might even be fun, being free, being really free to do whatever we wanted. Most people, they have responsibilities, like taking care of their family, having to work at a less-than-desirable job for pennies, begging for extra hours to feed a kid on the way. Luckily that wasn't Markus or me anymore, I was sitting there in my ex-girlfriend's dad's office, floored by what I had heard. I ignorantly mentioned, "You know, I would have took less, like way less." He smirked and said, "I've been in this business a long time, and this offer is unheard of, so why don't you shut up while we are both ahead."

As I sat in silence, Veronica's dad leaned over the desk, resting both elbows. "I assume this is something you're going to do. If you want help, I have several lawyers I can recommend, as well as accountants."

Accountants? I was struggling to buy bologna at the market the other day. How was it possible that I would need an accountant? Of all the things I thought I would never be able to experience, like sipping wine in an African country with vacation spots just a few miles from starving children, or having sex with a hairy French woman in a hotel with a view of the Eiffel Tower, or getting captured by the North Korean army while taking pictures too close to the border. Not once had I ever thought of the privilege of seeing someone crunch numbers for me. When I thought about it, it wasn't really fair. I mean, I was lucky, I was really lucky, and I could have easily just had to get another job, slaving away for someone who didn't know my name as he laughed to the bank. I really didn't deserve this luck at all, I hadn't done anything special, I wasn't good at anything, the only thing I did good was rent a less-than-expensive crack house. Cheap, I was good at being cheap. It's not like I had a lot of options though, but now the options would be limitless. I was about to be able to do whatever I wanted. If this were a dream, I would have killed myself for waking up.

I was excited to see Markus's reaction. I got home, closing the screen door loudly so Markus could hear.

He came out of his room, eating a bagel. "What's up?"

"I think we should talk," I said. Markus gulped in fear that it would be about the night we both would rather forget about.

"OK," he said.

We sat down in the living room, Markus slowly and awkwardly nibbling on the bagel. I could tell he thought it was going to be about the night in Bloomington, especially since I opened the conversation with Veronica's dad. Markus kind of just stared, not moving for a bit, as I did when I was told. He had bits of bagel in his mouth. "Uh, I don't want it," he said.

"Don't want what?" I said. As surely he wasn't talking about the money I just told him about I thought, but he was. "Why?" I asked.

"It's not mine, it's not yours either, it's his relatives, whoever they are," he said.

"He doesn't have any family. His last surviving family member was the old woman who lived in this house."

Markus stood up. "Well, I'm happy for you, but I'm moving to L.A., I don't have time for this." He then left the room.

I sat there, shocked. How could anyone not have time for two million dollars? I stood up and went after him, into his porn-poster room. "Tell me what I'm missing here? It's not making sense to me." He was changing clothes when I went in. It always amazed me how he could get naked right in front of people without caring. I guess that's why he was born to do porn.

He said to me in an angered way, "You can't keep me from following my dreams. Not you and not two million dollars!" I had never seen him stand up against me like this. I hadn't ever seen him confrontational towards me.

"I'm not trying to keep you from what you want to do, I'm trying to help you," I said.

"Help me? Help me for what?" Markus stammered.

"From struggling," I said.

This seemed to make him madder. "Struggle? You know, that book has you just so messed up that suddenly you think everyone has the same problems as you."

I couldn't believe he was getting mad at me. "You're acting like I'm handing you a hand grenade."

Something was troubling Markus as he sat down in his indoor lawn chair we saved from the neighbors' trash one day. He stared at his rug as if he couldn't look at me, as if he did, he would catch some debilitating disease. I wasn't far off with this thinking.

"I have HIV."

My face went pale as I could feel all the blood in my body rush to my legs. I stood there for a bit not knowing what to say.

"What?" I said.

"I got tested a few weeks ago, and again a week later to be sure. I'm HIV positive, Richard, and you probably are, too." I sat down on Markus's bed.

"You're for sure?" I asked.

"I don't know how much surer I could be," he said. "It's not as bad as it use to be, I've been seeing a doctor, and he's right, people live with it now. It's just not very easy. That basketball player caught it in the early nineties and he seems to be still doing well. You have to get tested though. If you have it then you need to take care of it as soon as possible," he said. "If you need help telling Veronica, I'll be there for you."

This was the first time the name Veronica had been mentioned while we were both in the room since that night in Bloomington. I wanted to deck him for her name even coming out of his mouth. This was all his fault, if he hadn't been such a disgusting slut, sleeping with everyone, I wouldn't of had this problem, Veronica wouldn't of had this problem.

I angrily said back, "You would just love that wouldn't you?" There was silence for a bit.

Then he said, "What are you talking about Richard? This is serious?" I was still looking at the floor trying to comprehend everything.

"You knew what you were doing."

"And I'm sure she did too, so what's your point?"

I stood up fast like and grabbed Markus by the collar, pushing him against the wall. Markus pushed back and pushed me against the mirror, cracking the mirror in two. I punched Markus partly on his cheek, and partly on his nose, blood spurted and bubbled out of his nostril everywhere, he let me go and we both fell to the ground. I went after him to punch him again, not thinking at all about my safety.

I see now that Markus cared more about me than I cared about myself. As I came after him and he yelled at me to stop, that he was bleeding, with all the screaming he was doing, I finally did. I stood up as he lay on the ground. Markus then stood up, looking me square in the eyes with anger as he wiped blood that ran down his mouth.

"You better hope you don't have this, because if you do, I'll finish you." Markus walked out leaving me standing in the middle of his room.

I looked at myself in the cracked mirror. The two sides of my face with a crack down the middle of the mirror was quite fitting. Although, at times, it seemed more like there were about seven sides to Richard Wright. The complexity of my life could have been made simple if I were only in my element, around the grass and trees. Life in these boxes has made it too complicated. Society was drowning me, I could either go up for air or let it consume me. If you've ever had one of those times where everything was so out of focus, which all you could do was ignore all your senses. That's what it was like for me in this moment. The stillness in the air, the look of sharp glass, capable of cutting my skin, the sound of a rattling car from outside the window, all this had to be ignored, because if it weren't, I would've exploded. It was almost if I had exchanged places with a ghost inside Markus's room. The terror of my life was inexcusable, and had to be dealt with.

I sat in my room that night not knowing what to tell Veronica, or her dad. Maybe, just maybe, I didn't have it, and maybe Veronica didn't either. What was I to do either way? I would never be able to forgive myself If Veronica was sick, or even worse, died. I needed to talk to her, but I didn't quite know how. This wasn't something to be told over a cell phone. Veronica's dad didn't want me to tell Veronica about our arrangement regarding Oliver's book, he thought it would be too awkward for her. I felt he was right, he basically didn't want to tell his daughter that her ex boyfriend was going to help make him even more filthy rich. Veronica having HIV, because of me, would be even worse.

How did I get into this mess? And how could I get out of it? I spent another night pacing back and forth around my cluttered room. I took out a secret stash of marijuana that I kept in my x box, the stash I told myself I would throw away before using again. I smoked it, and for the first time, things were calm, things were clear, somehow my brain wasn't worrying about what would happen or what I should do. All my senses were ignored again, and I fell asleep with my head hanging over the bed looking at infomercials on my television. It was that kind of sleep where my brain still took in the objects being sold to me for nineteen ninety-nine. I woke up thinking about little cups that crush and dice up peanuts. Within the minute, that thought had ended, and I was back to the feeling of dread and a broken spirit.

As pitiful as it sounds, I had to try and do this and still somehow get Oliver's book published with Veronica's dad. He was my only shot; I'm pretty sure every other publishing company in the world had rejected it so far. He didn't know that though, and if he had, the offer would've been much lower than it was. My conscious wouldn't let me tell Veronica after the book was published. If there was only some way to get Veronica tested without her knowing she was getting tested. Also, Markus needed to sign some paperwork with Veronica's dad. I questioned if Veronica's dad would be OK with me telling him that Markus didn't want anything to do with two million dollars. Probably not I thought. It was almost as if Veronica's dad wanted to help two of us out instead of one. As if he was spending a month doing good deeds, and he needed just two more to fill the quota, whatever the reason was, it felt like Markus wanting nothing to do with two million dollars wouldn't be enough for Veronica's dad, at least without him speaking to Markus first. Markus and Veronica's dad speaking was not a good option for me either. Markus was angry with me, and though I doubted that he would ruin this deal for me, it was just too big to risk. A thought that kept running through my head was Markus telling Veronica himself. This wouldn't be good either. I needed to sidestep around, and make a few things work in my advantage if everything was going to play out the way I wanted them to. Oddly, the possibility of me having HIV wasn't the biggest worry I had. Also, I despised needles, I would much rather die from aids then have to be stuck with one of those bruising needles. Then I decided that the first thing on my agenda was to smooth this over with Markus. It couldn't be that hard to get someone to split two million dollars could it? After, I would call Veronica and tell her that I had something like mono, and that I just wanted to make sure she didn't have it. I was sure the clinic would test Veronica's blood for everything. If she had it, they would tell her, their was no point in worrying her if she didn't have it, but I needed to make sure she actually got tested. Knowing Veronica, I figured she would just assume she didn't have mono because she wasn't feeling sick, and not get tested.

Maybe if I used magic and told her I loved her, she would definitely fall for that. I would have her under my spell again, though when using that magic spell this carelessly, it would be hard to cast a spell to get her out of it. It would be even harder for me to do it without getting killed by her woman hate glare. All women have it and usually reserve them for their own species. This time though, I would receive the glare, and probably several smacks to the face. It was beginning to sound like a bad idea. Realistically, I couldn't twist the knife in her back anymore. I figured it was about even, she had hurt me, and I was curious if I ever really hurt her, but either way, I couldn t do it, it just wasn't in me to do it.

I was beginning to feel like I was spending too much time thinking of ways to get out of it, and that I would just have to bite the speeding bullet and do it and let things just happen. The manipulation I was trying to achieve wasn't in my nature; it was something I had learned from living amongst people so long, it was about surviving amongst them. I didn't need it, or at least didn't want it. I was making this a big ordeal when it really didn't have to be. My imagination was telling me that all these things would happen as consequences of telling her. I was taking these consequences to be true, when in reality I had no idea what would really happen. Even though I kind of wanted it to, the world wasn't going to implode. Me and Veronica might have to take medication for the rest of our lives, but that's no biggie right? I was staring at death constantly when I looked in the mirror, my body could be a cesspool of disgusting viruses, knowing Markus's history. I decided, even though I would rather eat nails with mayonnaise, and I hate mayonnaise, to go ahead and get the needle in my veins to see if I had the debilitating disease of the eighties and nineties.

Every doctor around Indianapolis knew my dad, so I had to travel three hours west to Illinois. It was a quaint little town that was just dying for something to happen to it. Luckily, I was there with my HIV infested body. I got something to eat at the local diner and was curious to know what the elderly people drinking coffee would've thought if they knew they were sitting a few feet away from someone who probably has AIDS.

When I called the doctor's office to set up the appointment, I could tell from the reaction of the nurse on the other end that the town would be full of gossip after I went to get tested. She probably thought it was someone that lived amongst them, I'm sure she asked around if anyone knew a Richard Wright as soon as I had gotten off the phone.

I walked in with sunglasses and a bears hat that I had gotten at there one and only gas station. The nurses acted as professional as possible, but I knew as soon as I left the waiting room that the gossip would start up amongst all three of the thirty to forty year old nurses at this small private doctor s office that I think used to be a bank.

I was soon sitting in the doctor's chair, waiting for my arm to be bruised. I closed my eyes, clinched my teeth, and held on to the chair as if I were taking off into space. The worst part was when they actually pulled the blood out, that part is undeniably fucking painful. I had to wait a week and then they would call me.

I drove home through the night on a lonely highway into Indiana, rain fell on my Ford Explorer, I was still wearing the bears hat. I prayed to god that I didn't have HIV, and that Veronica didn't either. I hadn't prayed in a while; when I did, I always apologized for only praying when I needed something. I believe that there is a God, and whoever he is, he probably has his reasons for putting me on earth. It's just that at moments like this, we all need a little help. I smoked a cigarette to relieve the stress, I prayed for forgiveness for all the confusing things I had done. The only reason for doing them was the confusion on why I was alive. I hoped that he was listening, and that he could understand. Where would I be in five years? I wondered. Five years before this moment I was probably doing a double shift, selling baby booties. The stillness and boredom of driving down this road was beginning to be too much.

As I drove down the highway, something from my peripheral vision caught my eye; it was the first left turn I had seen in about an hour, and in an odd spot. I didn't know what it was, maybe because I had just prayed, but whatever it was, it was pulling my attention towards it. As I got closer I slowed down, I noticed a dirt path that led off into the woods. I sat there asking myself why the hell I was looking down this dirt path. I mean I was tired, I wanted to go home, why was I sitting in the middle of the night looking down this dirt path that led into darkness? It had to mean something, right? Whatever the reason was, more than likely desperation, I decided to follow. I drove deeper and deeper into the woods, I wondered if I was going crazy, but the more I pondered, the more I wanted to know what inevitable force was pulling me into these woods, and what was at the end.

Finally, after what seemed longer than it probably was, my headlights hit something at the end of the dirt path. It was nothing more than this old wood cabin. I got out of the Explorer and took a look. It looked to have been a vacation spot at one time, the roof had caved in though and it wasn't in living condition. I imagined at one time it must've looked like something that Oliver once lived in.

When I got closer to the door, I noticed a little sign with paint chipped away on it. It hung to the right of the door. I had to take the sign off of its nail and hold it to the explorer lights to see what it said. The first letter was unreadable and I could only make out "addyshack." Addyshack? I thought. What the hell is that? I didn't know why I turned off onto that dirt path, and after finding the wood cabin titled "addyshack." I definitely didn't know, I wouldn't fully understand till later.

The darkness that surrounded the wood cabin was frightening, it was far enough off the charts of society that no one would hear me if I screamed. It was time to get back in the explorer, as I didn't want to be the inspiration for the next Texas Chainsaw Massacre remake.

A few hours later I pulled into my driveway. My phone was vibrating and it was my new favorite person, Veronica's dad. I answered and he said, "You know, I know you're not a writer or anything, but I've only helped out about three people in my life like I'm helping out you. None of them took two days to call me back."

"I apologize, it hasn't been a pleasant two days. Markus doesn't want any part of the deal," I said.

"He doesn't, are you sure?" he replied.

"Pretty sure," I replied back.

"Don't be greedy son, you'll save more money from the legal problems later," he said.

"Well let me push a little bit harder, and I'll give you a call in a day or so," I said.

"Sounds good, talk to you then," he said.

We hung up and I sat in the driveway a little longer, contemplating my next step under a full moon. Maybe I'm just one of those people that can't find any good in anything. I was sitting on the edge of a life changing business deal, and all I thought about was the bleakness in my life. What ever happened to my disguise? I used to be able to put on a happy face; those days of playing with my Tonka trucks at age six were long gone. I scoured people with my eyes and wondered if they had a soul most times. The moon reflected off the windshield and made me wonder what I was doing in this body. I had sulked long enough and went inside to have another forgettable night alone.

I woke up expecting another silent day between me and Markus, at least until I spoke to him first. I awoke in my underwear and went into the hallway to go to the bathroom; I had to go so bad that I didn't have time to fully wake myself up. I stumbled into the hallway rubbing the sleep out of my eyes and ran into an already showered and awake Markus, he was going to work.

"Hey can we talk when I get back from work?" he asked.

"Uh sure," I said.

I was too tired to demand that he tell me at once what he wanted to talk about, which is what I would usually do. I can't stand waiting the whole day wondering what someone is talking about when they do that. It was too late though, and Markus was off to work, and I was pissing in the toilet, filling up the bowl and mixing our waste together, as if I was a scientist. I flushed and tried to go on about my day without too much wonder about what he wanted to talk about at five thirty when he gets home. I was sure I could deal with whatever curve ball he had now, the bastard probably had a real big one for me I thought. The way things were going I had to be prepared for anything. I just hoped he hadn't given me gonorrhea too.

We had a light bulb in the kitchen that was the magic light bulb, it seemed to last forever, I was trying to cook some eggs at about four thirty when the kitchen light bulb went out. I had to go and get a ladder from the neighbor and a pack of new light bulbs, and before I knew it, it was five thirty and Markus had walked into the kitchen with me standing on the ladder putting a new light bulb in. Markus leaned up against the doorway and shyly spoke.

"Look I talked to a doctor the other day, and we talked about my situation, I'm not going be able to really afford this disease. I'm not covered; I never could afford health insurance or anything. Anyways I would like to apologize, and to accept your offer if you still want to give it to me."

"If it wasn't for you we wouldn't have gotten in the attic at all. Plus, all I wanted to do was help you out; I mean you're my friend you know? And together I think we can survive this, or at least have a hell of a time before we kick the bucket." I smiled at him hoping he could see a brighter side to everything, he couldn't.

"Yeah, I don't know," he said.

I looked at him and saw that he was scared, maybe it hadn't hit me like him because I still had hope that I didn't have I it. He responded in a way I never saw.

"I just never really thought about dying before, it always seemed like something that wasn't real before all this."

I got down from the ladder, putting the light bulbs in the cupboard.

"It doesn't seem quite fair does it?" I responded.

"I guess it's better that I die sooner than later since I won't ever be able to do what I really wanted to," he said.

I hadn't thought about it, but I realized that not only would this disease possibly take away his life, but also it would take away his only passion for life, porn. As silly as porn is to me or anybody else, it was horrible to see his passion for life vanquished. I could only look at him with wonder, the only thing I ever felt like I was meant to do was get Oliver's book published. That was about to happen, I never thought about what I would do after, I didn't have a plan and definitely didn't feel I was born to do anything.

I wanted to hug him and tell him everything would be OK, but I couldn't. There is something in the heterosexual man's genes that won't let him show emotion for other men. Then on the other hand, maybe it was just being a part of the pro patriarchy, male dominated, hunter and gatherer society, which made a man feel like he couldn't hug another man. I was worried about him, but what could I do? I was starting to think I needed to worry about myself now.

I thought about the possibility of me never being able to find what I was born to do. There was a high chance I could be dead before that, I needed to start taking that seriously. Every time my phone rang my nerves would get all built up. I was hoping that it was a call with the results of my test; it would make me heat up and get into a sweat. Usually it was just my dad or mom who I still hadn't told about any of this.

Then on a Friday morning, I finally got the call; I could tell it was them by the Illinois area code.

"Richard Wright?" the nurse asked.

"Yes," I replied. I could feel the sweat ready to come out of my pours. My temperature had to have gone up in the instant of the call. It was something I wish I could've had scientific proof of, but my temperature had to of went up to a hundred and five with in seconds.

"We have your results, you tested negative for HIV," the nurse said.

"Negative?" I asked. "Is that good or bad?"

"Good, It means you don't have HIV," the nurse said. I bit my index finger hard with happiness.

"Thank you so much!" I said.

"If you have any questions feel free to give us a call," the nurse said.

I was so relieved, I laid my face down on the floor so happy as I prayed to God, sure that he had heard me. It had to have been some kind of supernatural force for me not to be infected with the disease, I thought. My eyes closed, my cheek bones laid on the stained carpet, I thought of how strange I was, expressing my overwhelming excitement, as if I was almost scared of someone hearing me. In fact, when I think of it now, I was, it was almost a halfhearted relief for myself. I still had my only friend sick with the disease.

After the talk with Markus, I almost felt like I needed to have the disease so that me and Markus could cope with it together, but now Markus had to cope with it alone. I was feeling optimistic about Veronica's chances, although I wondered if it was a mistake. I was still wondering how I would go about it. I knew I couldn't just call her to set up a time to speak; she might get the wrong impression.

I borrowed my mother's car, it was a white Chevy Impala, and I took out anything that would be noticeable to Veronica as it being my mother's car. I put black furry dice on the rearview mirror to give the impression of a completely different person. I would hope that anyone reading this will not think I'm a creep after confessing what I'm about to confess, but I parked my mother's car down her street and tried to catch her going somewhere so I could follow her and pretend that we ran into each other. The first day I did this there was no luck, her car didn't move all day, and I ended up wasting about six hours of my time listening to AM radio.

I went back the next morning and finally saw her get into her yellow mustang. She drove and I stayed back away as I could tell she was going into town. She stopped off at a Starbucks and went inside. I parked my mother's car a good distance away from hers and decided to go in. I wanted to make it look like I was going in when she was going out, so the timing had to be right. I had binoculars that I bought for thirty dollars and was upset because I didn't think I would have the opportunity to use them for my stakeout. I looked into Starbucks and saw that she was making her way out with her tall hot chocolate. I went for it. I kept my head down to make it seem more natural. As we got closer to each other in this large parking lot that was shared with the city mall, I could tell that she noticed me but was just going to walk past me.

"Hey?!" I said optimistically. She didn't respond and just kept walking with those huge sunglasses covering her face. I ran towards her, walking next to her as she began to speed up towards her car.

"Hey how are you?" I asked. She still had no response as she began to move closer to her car. "You're not going to speak to me now?" I said.

"Nope, go away," she said.

Veronica got into her car. As she did, I told her that I needed to speak with her, but she was playing it like I wasn't there. Which was understandable, but I needed to make sure she didn't have it. I decided I needed to stop playing around and to just call her. I went to my mother's car and called her cell several times, no answer. That was almost even more of a surprise, I figured she would at least answer once to tell me to stop calling.

I went home that night, it was ten PM and I hadn't gotten anything out of Veronica. Then I get a call from Veronica's dad's office. I pick up and immediately said, "Hey me and Markus will be in tomorrow to sign the paperwork." Veronica's dad was a little surprised but seemed happy.

"Oh great, try to come by noon, and I'll introduce you to the publisher," Veronica's dad said.

"Ok," I said.

"Did you see Veronica today?" he asked.

"Yeah, at Starbucks," I said.

"You weren't going to tell her about our deal were you?"

"No, not at all," I said.

"Great I would like to handle that if possible", he said.

"Yeah um I would like to talk to her though," I said.

"Really? What about?" He pried and I stuttered uncomfortably. I was about to make something up like how I still have her coat or something like that when he interrupted me.

"Because I don't think she wants to talk to you, or Markus, ever again."

I squinted my eyes, trying to figure out what that meant. Did he somehow know? Did she tell him? If she did, then does her dad just not care? Or was his fifteen percent of the book deal the bottom line here? I wouldn't find out until years later, but his house, the cars, the luxurious lifestyle, was all for show. I found out later that he was in over his head in debt at this time, and the book deal would merely break him even again, if he used all of it to pay the debt off, which from what I heard he did. I was feeling more comfortable about going in to sign the papers for some reason. Now that he knows, there's nothing to hide. I put off telling Veronica, for at least the day I thought.

I introduced Markus to Veronica's dad. From there he took us to the publisher. It was a nicely sized publishing house on the top floor of a business building. The carpets were styled yellow, the lights were dimmed and everyone had an office with see through windows as walls and a door. We walked past a display of some cooking book they were coming out with; some Martha Stewart look alike was on the cover. They seemed pretty successful although the books they had published I had never heard of, which wasn't a surprise, I didn't really read.

Me and Markus sat down and they went over the entire mind numbing business details that a lawyer should be doing, and that's exactly who we told them to speak to. Me and Markus decided to split the costs and share a lawyer. They also mentioned that the local news would like to speak with us, I was a tad bit worried about that as was Markus. They were pretty intent on it happening, though. As they said, it was an opportunity for the national news to take notice as well as giving the book a high-profile status before it was even published.

One thing I liked that they said was that they weren't going to merely re-type Oliver's words into a computer and print it out. They were actually going to make copies of Oliver's original handwriting and try to make the book look as authentic as possible to the actual thing. They wanted every book to look old, dusty, and dingy so that for everyone who bought the book it would seem like they found it up in some old attic too. They also asked me and Markus to write the forward in the front of the book that included our story of how we found it. They were going to hire a writer to help us do that, and it sounded fantastic to both of us. Though Markus seemed like he couldn't really focus, and who could blame him? It didn't seem like we were really supposed to be in this office. We came in our dress up clothes; button up shirts and jeans from the local mall. This was all just casual clothes to these people.

They were making the cheddar, which really made me wonder why they were publishing the book. So I asked. The answer wasn't surprising. They thought that they could make a lot of money. I wondered why the few publishing companies that read it passed on it. Maybe they were just stupid when it came to being greedy. I knew they were in fact greedy. What I would come to find out is that there is a little bit of greed in all of us. It's in our nature just as it's in a monkey's nature to love bananas.

Weeks passed and the sickness called depression soon ended with Markus and I both. I think it happened when the check cleared. We decided to continue to live together, to move out of the crack house we called home, and to buy a new home together. We seriously thought about moving to California, but as much as we hated Indiana, the reality of leaving to California just made us want to stay in the corn state that much more. We also realized that two million dollars wouldn't take us that far in California, not like it would in Indiana.

We bought a house for around two hundred thousand dollars, a house that probably would of cost about ten million in California. We went home and sat in the living room of our rented crack house and were both just quiet for a while as we thought about things, then suddenly, we looked at each other and started laughing and screaming, and talking about how much fun this was going to be. We stood on the well-pedicured lawn of our new house in a gated community just outside Indianapolis. It was brick with clear glass windows where you could see the living room from outside. It was gigantic compared to anything that Markus had ever lived in. Most of the time I felt like I was just in a new house that my parents had bought, it didn't really feel like I would've ever been able to buy a house like this if it weren't for Oliver's book. I had always hoped that one day I could be successful like my dad, it just, probably wasn't ever going to happen.

The house had all-white stone floors. We tried buying our own furniture but it just started to be too random. I took down the number of my psychiatrist's interior designer. Who cares? I thought modern things are expensive, and expensive things make the vaginas wet. I was just surprised that at the end of the day somehow it matched. Markus wanted to feel like he was home, and me coming off a break up, wanted a bachelor pad that would be ready for sexual escapades at any time, especially from strippers that we would decide to take back. Honestly, the place would've made strippers put out no matter what the inside looked like, the outside did its job, and it said that Markus and Richard were stacked.

The book was taking time at the publishing house before it was released. Meanwhile, me and Markus picked up a fun little activity at strip clubs; it was called getting as many as possible to put out in the "COKEHOUSE" as we called it. Obviously we were above living at a house with the stigma of crack, and had moved on to better things, like a house that could only be viewed as a drug king pin's residence. We bought tons and tons of expensive clothes from Banana Republic that really seemed to help out. I was beginning to feel like the poor douche bag I hit with the alcohol bottle. By the way, I not only paid for his surgeries but I also sent him thirty grand for college. I had heard around the grapevine his parents couldn't afford it anymore, that he was working as a cashier at a gas station. I felt really, really better about myself after that. I questioned if I should've gave him more, but I felt like the best thing to do for him was to pay for his college. If I had given him money just for the hell of it he would've bought a Hummer. He was young just like me, and hell, I bought a Hummer. I didn't really think about what a waste of money it was.

All this expensive stuff I used to see, as a waste was something I soon felt like I needed. I had bought the prior year's Hummer a few months before the new one came out, and when it did, I felt like I needed the brand new version of the Hummer. The last year's version wasn't good enough for Richard Wright. Before, all I wanted was freedom, now all I wanted was more new expensive stuff.

I had lived a year with Markus partying every night, drunk every night, staying up all night, having fun all night, and never once thought about anything else. I came home one day from staying over at my new girlfriend's house. Her name was Emma. She was seventeen, rich, and yes, still living with her parents. I parked my black Hummer with iced rims on me and Markus's driveway. I walked toward the lawn with a hangover from the previous night. Markus was laying out in his swimming shorts with two strippers we had become friends with. No, Markus didn't have sex with them. Well, I had always questioned if he did this one time, but they both knew he was infected and for the most part just gave him hand jobs and condom-covered blowjobs. Markus seemed to be doing fine, he was taking a lot of medication, and apart from a few weeks of throwing his guts up, he was pretty OK.

The book was about to be released, finally. I never knew how much time and effort went on behind publishing a book. I never knew how many people worked on them too. They spent a lot of money on getting the book ready. Also, we started to get a little famous too, locally anyways. Exactly one week from the moment of standing on the lawn while Markus sunbathed with our two stripper friends, we were both due to be on The Today Show. We didn't know who would be interviewing us, either Matt Lauer or Al Roker, to the two of us we didn't care, they were both awesome. I had remembered waking up early in the morning getting ready for high school, and in between getting ready I would watch The Today Show with my parents. Now I too will have one of these two bastards interviewing me.

Well I don't know how to tell you what I was feeling, excited and drunk I guess.

"We gotta wake up early Sunday morning to catch our flight. No wild craziness the night before."

The two strippers we had met were ironically named Monica and Rachel. They looked nothing like their counter parts Courtney Cox and Jennifer Anniston. No, Monica and Rachel were actually hotter, hard to imagine but it's true. Yeah I guess you could say that being rich had made me forget about the skanks. Monica on the right side of Markus, was blonde, tight body and model thin, she somehow had a nice big ass though. I know too, because I went balls deep in it, twice. It hurt too much for me do it again. Her friend Rachel though, actually enjoyed anal sex, and her ass was just as fine. Rachel had a D cup though which made the pleasure that much better; she was also way thicker which I liked. After reminding Markus of our flight, Rachel looked on with a serious demeanor.

"But what are we going to do?"

Monica and Rachel were very high maintenance, and me and Markus both had the money to spend. But there were no attachments, at least with us. Them on the other hand were probably more so as time went on, at least that was what we secretly hoped.

"Is it first class?" Markus asked.

"Yeah, It should be, I won't fly anything else, not in these times of terror. If your gonna be flown into a building, why not go first class."

Rachel jealously asked, "How's Emma?"

I replied, "Emma's fine. How are you?"

She replied, "Bored, you wanna entertain me?" Rachel was the reason I turned into a magnificent lay and I felt like for the first time I was addicted to something. That something was her sex. It's hard to imagine being addicted to someone's sex. Me and Markus had tried every drug under the sun since we had become wealthy enough to do so, I didn't have a problem kicking any of them. I questioned if Markus was still taking Vicodin. But Rachel, her sex made me think I should check into rehab. She was a dirty girl by all accounts, she moaned and begged, whether it was in one hole or the other.

Markus started his career as a porn director. Rachel and Monica were in his first movie. Technically so was I but no one would ever know, I told Markus not to show my face, which really isn't a problem in porn I guess. Markus didn't really take his first taping with me too seriously and I was pretty sure he just trashed the tape, most of it was Monica and Rachel laughing as I tried to have sex with both of them.

I played the usual games that girls in high school played with me (a lot of good those college classes did me), but only with Emma. I told her that Rachel, Monica, and me were just friends. I was Emma's first love, so she bought everything I said. I was sure that soon enough she would realize that she was young, and that no, we weren't going to be together forever. I had actually met Emma when she was waiting to see my dad at his doctor's office, who by the way had been pretty neutral about all of this. He pretended to be happy for me at times, but my mother was more excited for me than he was. I guess because I hadn't really done anything besides collect a check. I think he thought I didn't deserve it, and lately I was beginning to wonder myself.

Emma was in the waiting room, she was wearing all brown knee-high leather boots, a dress, and an over coat, which was her usual attire. I said something to her, I believe it was for her to pass me a magazine, and she just kept talking, so I eventually got her number and we had been dating ever since. As I had sex with Rachel on my three thousand dollar bed, silk sheets, silk pillowcases, for the first time, I legitimately began to feel really undeniably bad about what I was doing. With Veronica I always kind of just told myself that this was wrong, but didn't really believe it. I don't know, Emma was just so innocent. Yes, I would think to myself that there is no possible way to ever know that she was totally being faithful, and that yes she was only in high school. Yes she was probably flirting with the high school halfback and doing whatever else, maybe even fooling around just as much as me.

For some reason, as I unenthusiastically turned Rachel over on her stomach, I started thinking for the first time since my life had changed so dramatically. A while back I had gotten an email from Veronica to meet for lunch, I guess I had some stuff at her place that she wanted to give back. I figured this would be some ploy to get me back. It wasn't. We met at an outside diner, she showed up with dark sunglasses on as if she had been crying, maybe it was just wishful thinking on my part though.

She hadn't really emailed me to pick up my stuff, not really anyways. I mean she knew I had my own toothbrush and shampoo, OK maybe I wanted my DVD package of The Godfather, but at this point I could've bought a new one. We didn't talk about the book, or her father's involvement in it, which at this point I'm sure she knew. No, what she brought me there to tell me was that she was sick, I had put off telling her, I figured she was fine, I mean I was fine, why would the universe let me off the hook and not Veronica? She brought me there to tell me that she had AIDS, and that I should get checked out.

How awkward this must of been for her. I couldn't bring myself to tell her, I felt awful for not caring enough. She at least did, she cared enough to tell me when she found out, why couldn't I have done the same? I had a hangover the night before from partying, and I felt nothing for her. No sympathy, no compassion, even though I was the one that had a hand in this, I had done this to her, I had Markus sleep with her that night. All I could do at the time was jealously think of whom she thought she got it from.

After she told me, and I stared at her as she cried for what seemed to be an endless amount of moments, she spoke, "Please don't make me tell Markus, please."

I nodded, little did she know, he knew all too well about it, and so did I. I was a horrible person. I was born so self-centered. The money had made it worse; I just couldn't believe that a person I basically grew up with meant nothing to me. She was sick, it was my fault, and yet that day when she told me, I didn't care. I didn't care for months until I started banging Rachel doggy style, I have no idea why of all moments it was that moment, but it was.

Veronica was so scared of what I thought of her, I could tell by the way she avoided eye contact. She said she missed me, and I just stared at her some more, unforgiving to her and her time for need. Veronica wasn't perfect, but neither was I, we didn't belong together, but she deserved my respect, I wish I could've given it to her. I began to feel like I couldn't do this anymore. It had been a slow progression but finally I had come to a point where I would rather take a knife to the back from someone, then do it to them. Emma would write me little love emails while she was at school; buy me teddy bears just because. It seemed like she genuinely loved me, if she didn't she was doing a pretty good job at hiding it. Even so, I didn't care; I could not ever do this to anyone again. I grew limp as I pumped it inside of Rachel.

"Did you cum inside me?" she asked.

I didn't exactly want to disappoint her, so I said I did.

I lay down beside her, both of us hot, naked, and sweaty. We were laying in luxury, a stone statue head of Thomas Jefferson was staring at us at the end of the room, I had bought it just because, without a thought of anyone struggling like I once was.

"I wanna go shopping," Rachel said. I merely looked at her out of the corner of my eye. I questioned if I should ask it but I did anyways.

"If me and Markus didn't have money, would you still be around us?"

The truth was that I cared about these girls, even without the sex we had hung out and had some wild nights together, they were fun, it was fun being with them, I genuinely wanted them to be OK, and wanted them always to be in contact, no matter what happened. Rachel turned her head towards me and looked me in the eyes.

"Probably not," she said. I didn't expect it, but I appreciated the honesty, I figured that I would at least have to cipher out the truth from a lie she would tell me. It was hard to imagine that Rachel and Monica didn't feel the same way; we had spent so much time together. Living in America there is only one thing on your mind besides sex and food, it's the dollar bill, how to make it, how to find it, how to get two wealthy dumb guys who found a book to spend it.

I shouldn't have been as surprised about the answer; there had been something different about Rachel for a few weeks. I was beginning to see what it was, it was a conscious, we had both grew one, and in an odd way, we both grew one together. It made me wonder what was going on in the lives of Markus and Monica.

Markus and I flew down to New York, and were both deadly nervous to be on TV. The flight over would've been fine if it weren't for a toddler kicking the back of my chair like a soccer ball. Even in first class life can be intolerable. I would've loved to yank that kid out of his chair by his hair, along with his mother that probably thinks her child can do no wrong, and send them out of the plane with gaping holes in their parachutes.

The luxuriousness of the room we stayed in made me ill, who really deserves this life anyways? Why did the guy asking for change by the hotel door deserve that life? It's all just kind of unfair and cruel. Even though me and Markus were scared of being on television, we were also ready, we had spent at least half of the entire advance we had gotten in the past year, and were ready to start collecting royalties.

It was a big day; we woke up super early, earlier than usual since it was a morning show. We sat in a room called the green room, but the room wasn't really green, which made me and Markus both think for a bit. We weren't the only guests that day; Tom Cruise was also a guest. Markus and I watched on the television in the green room as we ate pastries, when suddenly the interview with Matt Lauer and Tom cruise began to go sour. Suddenly me and Markus were too enamored about what was taking place to keep eating. The producer had told us that we would be on after Mr. Cruise at eight thirty. Well eight thirty came, and that's when the guy from "Top Gun" called Matt Lauer glib. There was actually more material of the interview that they actually edited out that made the interview way longer, but the time slot we had, had suddenly gone and passed.

The producer came out and apologized and told us that we would have to set up an appointment for next month. The producer kept apologizing like me and Markus were somebody important. The publishing company was furious, so much so that the re-scheduling for another interview never happened. The book was to be out soon, and then before we knew it, we woke up one day and it was. No review in the New York Times, no reviews anywhere, no one had heard of this book. We were getting ready to celebrate the rather small release that we naively thought was bigger.

Meanwhile, the pleasure of being rich enough to do anything was starting to get quite boring. Before there were many obstacles in my life that took creativity to make things work. When you're wealthy you can just throw money at your problems and for the most part they just go away. The comfort of the ten room mansion we were living in was beginning to get too unnatural for me, like a beast being kept in a zoo, a really luxurious zoo. A lot of days I just hung out by myself. Rachel and Monica were still always around, we had fun, even though they were greedy little sluts. I had gold silk pillows I could lose myself in. My bed was the most comfortable thing I probably will ever sleep in again. It was custom made by a Iranian man that did several other sofas and beds in the neighborhood, he said that his secret was that he had a genie stuff it for me, with what I had to pay him, he better of.

If there was ever something wrong with the mansion, or any of the toys we had, it was fixed. We had the ability to live in perfection, so we did. I couldn't really think about the people that didn't have money, it was hard to put myself back there even though it was just a short time ago when we were the ones that didn't have enough money for groceries. Markus forgot about it quick and never looked back, I think we were having too much fun to think.

Markus, me, Monica and Rachel would go out, get drunk and sometimes stop in at the local grocery store and find someone our age or older just trying to survive, people worse off then we were, sometimes with kids, and then, I saw someone who I recognized but couldn't quite put a finger on it. I then took a look at her kid and I knew who she was. It was late at night and Monica, Rachel and Markus were in another line laughing and carrying on. It was the plump twenty-three year old, probably now twenty four or five year old MILF regular I use to masturbate to while she was buying diapers for her kid. She was standing in front of me at the grocery store digging in her purse for change just trying to buy some pepper loaf, wheat bread, and mayonnaise. I was standing there wearing a four hundred dollar overcoat, with a two hundred dollar pair of shoes; I had become a sheep and hadn't realized it. She looked like she was having a hard day; she pounded her fist in front of the store clerk when she couldn't find the three dollars and fifty-seven cents she needed. I didn't want to embarrass her, I knew that if I was in the same situation just a short while ago, that I wouldn't be able to take the money if someone offered it.

"What's your name? Do you remember me?" I asked. She looked at me.

"Hi, my name's Cheryl, and no I don't remember you, and before you ask, no, I don't want your help." Cheryl quickly grabbed the mayonnaise and walked away to put it back. The store was empty since it was about three am, so I brought my sixty dollar bottle of wine that I had grew too accustomed to and followed her.

"Stop, stop, stop," I Said.

She turned around, sweaty with frustration and said, "What?"

I looked around, as I didn't quite know how to put it, so I grabbed the mayonnaise and said, "You just can't eat pepper loaf without the mayonnaise OK? It doesn't work."

She tried not to smile and just sort of looked at me with a whatever face. She walked back up to the cashier and let me pay; I took her home after I dropped off Markus, Rachel and Monica. She thanked me as she got out. What she didn't know was that when I helped her put her last bag of groceries inside, I went back to my hummer and wrote a check for three thousand dollars, along with a note that said if she didn't cash this check, I would be greatly offended. We had exchanged numbers and she called me before she cashed it, to be sure that she wasn't dreaming.

I felt really, really good about that. It was hard for me to even keep a thousand dollars at one time in my bank account, I was always just a few paychecks away from being homeless, but even then I had my wealthy parents to fall back on, a lot of people don't. From what she told me she worked as a clerk at a gas station that didn't give her many hours, a slave no different than I or Markus not long ago, only she had a little girl to take care of. She was barely surviving, she wouldn't ever get lucky and find a gold mine of a book like me, and she didn't have a doctor for a father to fall back on. She made one bad decision, having a kid before she was ready; she dropped out of community college because she didn't have the time or the money.

I left her house as the mist of the morning started to show and the grass had begun to frost. I got home teary eyed. For the first time I felt good about something I had done with my life, whether or not my father would ever know, he should've been proud of me for at least doing what I did that night. It was true that I was wealthy by luck, but so were a lot of people. What I did that night wasn't luck, and I wanted to keep this feeling going, it was better than buying a ton of unnecessary comfort objects like I had been doing.

The next day came and it was finally time to see the final copy. I was pleased, but it didn't seem to matter, the book only sold roughly three thousand copies. The plan the publishing company had to market the book relied almost solely on The Today Show and what kind of publicity they could achieve after. From what I understand now, the only reason we received the interview in the first place was because of a close friend of a friend the company had, neither me nor Markus knew it then. Me and Markus started being extra conservative with our cash flow. We didn't ever want to turn to selling our labor, being slaves again after having the kind of lifestyle we had come so accustomed to.

I sent an email to the publishing company asking what had happened, and why the book wasn't getting bought. I got an email back from the assistant of the president of the company that said. "Unfortunately, this is a sad truth to this business. We all expected great things, for it to be a hit, but when you get to the bottom line of it, no one reads anymore." I could only think to myself yeah, you're right, I don't read anything myself. Maybe I should've made it into a screenplay in hopes that Brad Pitt would play Oliver. That seemed to be the only way anything ever worked, Brad Pitt or some flash in the pan had to be in it. Robert Pattinson would be perfect, besides the fact that no one will know who he is next month, and him being Caucasian could be a problem too, someone still would've made it regardless of their race, all they would've seen was green.

The revolution wasn't going to happen anytime soon, I needed to conserve what capital I had and probably sell my half of the house to Markus if he still wanted it. I woke up early one morning after laying in bed for a few weeks, I received an email that the first royalty check had come in, and it was a whopping four thousand dollars. I told Markus as he lay out in the sun to see if he wanted to go with me to collect it, but he was very unenthusiastic about it after I told him how much it was. I walked into the publishing company with the feeling that this would be the last time I would ever come into the place again. I sighed and continued down the hall, I was just about to tell the secretary of Bob Herman's that I had arrived when I heard some overwhelming screaming from his office.

Bob was the one that had been dealing with us on a daily basis. I asked the secretary what was going on, she had known me for a while now and looked concerned and said, "You're gonna have to talk to Bob when you get in there."

The secretary walked into Bob's office and more screaming began. I waited for a bit longer and then the secretary came out flustered. I asked what was wrong.

She huffed and puffed and said, "This woman has been here all morning, I shouldn't be telling you this but she's Oliver's ancestor."

My mouth opened and I couldn't close it. Oliver's ancestor finally walked out, she was a very dark black woman with short hair and a pink Juicy jumpsuit on. She was holding a baby and walked right past me out of the building, very frustrated. I couldn't help myself, so of course I had to follow her. Bob's secretary came after me to try to stop me. She should have just saved her breath, because I wasn't about to listen.

I drove thirty minutes, anxious for the black woman to stop so that I could talk to her. We began to enter a neighborhood I had never been in before. Suddenly it was like the streets had died, as if street sweepers didn't exist in this neighborhood. I also noticed the familiarity of a pattern I was seeing; I had only seen it on MTV during the gangsta rap hour of videos, when they still played videos, that is. I saw gun store, liquor store, gun store, liquor store, church, and gun store. This was a time I hoped my tanned complexion could help me out. The Hummer I was driving and the clothes I was wearing definitely wouldn't.

She was driving an old seventies Cadillac that had been somewhat refurbished, the somewhat niceness of her car made me think that possibly she was doing OK, that possibly she didn't need money that bad. When we got to her house, I could tell I was wrong. It was a long street of low-income houses with mostly black people walking around and hanging out on the porches. I parked a bit far from her house, I didn't really know what I should do as I was driving my Hummer. Soon, I just didn't care; I had to speak with her. If it weren't for her family bloodline so many years ago, I wouldn't have gotten the chance to worry about my Hummer being stolen in the first place.

As I walked to the house, there was a guy with dreadlocks that looked at me like he was either going to rape me or kill me, apparently he thought I was here for other reasons as he asked, "You buying?"

I shook my head and quietly said no as I continued to walk with quickness to my step. What was funny about this was that I had probably seen a handful of black people in my entire life growing up in Indiana. Then suddenly I discovered a neighborhood that was like Africa, something I hadn't ever seen before. I walked up the steps to the porch and felt the weakness of the floorboards in the wood, which was very old. I wonder if I had eaten breakfast that morning if the floorboards would have cracked and if I would have fallen through.

I rang the doorbell and the "Jingle Bells" song played inside the house. I waited for a bit and then she answered. Her name was Bernice Earl. We sat inside, she brought me some lemonade and then she told me her story. This wasn't the first run-in with her family and this publishing company. Her great grandmother had seen if the publishing company would have been interested in publishing the book a great while ago. From what I understand they were, they just weren't interested in making a deal with a black family from the ghetto, and had originally offered them something so low that it offended her grandmother.

Berenice's family tried several times to get the memoirs published just like I had, they even had an agent at one time. For the most part no one was interested; the closest they got was with the publishing company that had purchased it from me and Markus. The publishing company had known about them all along from what I was told, it was hard to imagine, but Bernice later brought out her certified family tree. It kind of surprised me that somehow she was able to have a certified family tree, but if you followed her name down to the end, there he was, Oliver Earl. How a professional was able to track her ancestry to Oliver was beyond me. It was also on her driver's license, and her Social Security card: Bernice Earl.

This was in fact Oliver Earl's ancestor, and I had arrogantly been spending her money, the money she could have used to get out of the dump she lived in, the money she could have used to move to a neighborhood where grown men didn't offer to sell you drugs before you walked inside. I grew very angry about her situation but she told me not to, that she had gotten angry enough with Bob Herman and the publishing company that morning.

I sat quietly for a bit in front of her on her couch that was probably handed down to her from the seventies. I looked out at the sun that started to gaze in at me. She wasn't asking for anything, but she had nothing, nothing for her two toddlers that were running around playing, and nothing for her baby that she was holding. She didn't have a husband, and they didn't have a father. She was surviving the only way she knew how, she slept with men from time to time, men in her neighborhood, men that she loathed, and in return they would help with groceries, rent, and clothes. I could only sit and think about what Oliver would be thinking, there's no doubt in my mind that he wouldn't have ever imagined that one of his future granddaughters would have been selling her body from time to time.

This was America, and this is what it had become since it was founded, people surviving by any means necessary. She was a conventional slave as well, she worked nights as a security guard, most nights her kids would go unwatched because she just plain couldn't afford it. Bernice was glad that I had gotten the memoirs out there, she believed as I did that it was important for the American people to have access to it. I couldn't bare to tell her that the American people seemed to have no intention of actually reading it. Maybe in another decade though, maybe it would reach the American conscious then, and maybe the American people would finally know what finger to put up in front of their American bosses. The jury wasn't out on the memoirs yet, and even though I knew the reality of it, I still had hope.

I didn't know how to leave Bernice's with the clothes on my back that her great, great ancestor to about the tenth degree, had basically bought me. Bernice assured me that whatever decision I chose to make would be OK, but that she had to provide for her children, and that she would be sending a subpoena to my residence and the publishing company. I couldn't blame her, but I wanted to tell her about the truth the American judicial system, since me and Markus had all the money, and the fact that she could barely afford electricity, she didn't stand a chance in hell. I didn't want to discourage her though.

I also didn't really want to tell her that by copyright law, she would pretty much lose no matter how much money she had, the material wasn't technically hers or her family's anymore. It had been over two hundred years. The memoir went into the public domain quite a while ago, and no one from her family ever went to any trouble to copyright it them selves. Besides that fact though, it was just wrong what I was doing, I had gotten lucky when one way or another someone from the family had left it behind. A lot of people probably think that it should be finder's keepers, but when you're talking about the difference in lifestyle the two of us had; I just could tell that I wouldn't be able to live with myself if I didn't do something about it.

So I sat in my Hummer that Oliver basically bought me from writing the troubles of his life down on paper nearly two hundred years ago and I gave the predicament some thought. Even though it had been just a short while since my life had changed dramatically from one extreme to another, I still wasn't really happy. I didn't know if I would ever be happy, but I wanted to do what was right, that seemed to be the only thing anymore that could make me happy. What seemed right for me was to get away, from people, from buildings, from slavery. I didn't want to go back to killing myself just to make a buck, which was for sure. The more I thought about it, the more I knew I didn't need the Hummer, I didn't need the big screen TVs, I didn't need the excessiveness of any object. All I needed was food and water, everything else I owned seemed to own me, and what it made me do was work, it made me spend hours and days and years of my life I wouldn't get back. It wasn't worth it.

I sat there thinking about Markus, he wasn't going to be happy about what I was going to do. He was rather blind to all this, and would be content working if he had to. I also knew that he would be totally content with spending the money once he found out that it wasn't his. On the other hand though, his medication had quite a large bill at the end of the month. As it stood when all this went down, the government didn't care whether Markus was sick, and the health insurance companies, they definitely didn't care, they all just cared if he had enough money to pay for his sickness. Hopefully one day that will all change as well, and people will start caring about people, instead of just money. That's neither here nor there.

I needed to do what was right, so I decided to make a deal with Bernice. I walked back up to her porch, she was dressed in her security guard outfit, and I told her, "I'm gonna sign the money over to you, I just want to make sure that you're fine with me keeping enough to make sure my friend stays in good health. He's sick-"

Before I could explain the rest to her, her chin began to quiver and then she hugged me. I knew then that I was doing the right thing, for her and her family and for me and Markus too, he just didn't take it all that well.

A limestone lamp in my living room flew across the room and into the wall after I sat on the leather couch and told Markus. I had gotten him out of the pool for a serious talk; he probably had no idea that I was about to tell him this. "She let us keep enough money for any medical expenses," I told him.

"Let us? Let us? It wasn't hers to begin with."

"No, Markus, we were lucky enough to find it, that's it, we've had a good run but it's time to do what's right," I said.

"Are you out of your mind?! What are we going to do? We can't keep this place now, do you understand that?!" Markus said.

"Markus, you would have done the same thing, these people need this money more than we do! And it's not even ours! It's there's! And we are the ones living the life they should be!" I said.

There was some silence as Markus paced, he calmed down and then sat across from me. He put his head in his hands as if to guard himself from the answer to his next question.

"What are we going to do?" he asked. I sighed and told him.

"Look, the royalty checks aren't going to be padding our bank account like we thought anyways, we would've had to think of something sooner or later."

"I would have preferred later," he said.

"Me too, but it's not ours. Maybe if I hadn't read Oliver's book I could've put it out of my head and not cared... I did though and I do care," I said.

I could tell Markus wasn't looking forward to the change we were going to have to make, but he agreed finally and could only say, "Yeah."

We didn't talk the next few days. We both kind of walked around the mansion we once coveted so much as if it was on its deathbed. I would walk into a room and think, this will be one of the last times I'll be in here, and then go over the various memorable moments I spent in the room.

Monica and Rachel were like other coveted toys we weren't that excited about giving up. They were like the dirt bikes we bought, only we used Monica and Rachel more than two days, and we didn't put them in the garage after we were done. I would try putting them out of my head. Thinking about what would happen to our relationships without money wasn't exactly intriguing, so I would think about baseball or golf. Thinking about any mundane sport was better; sometimes I would watch a little ESPN, hoping that Chris Berman would take my mind off of Rachel and Monica. Then I would flip through the channels, and inevitably I would hear the theme song, "When rain starts to fall, I'll be there for you, like I once was there before." I couldn't help but watch, it was Friends and it seemed to be constantly on as I tried to put Rachel and Monica out of my mind.

It was kind of bullshit the more I thought about it. The Rachel and Monica characters from Friends would still be there for us without money, I mean, it said so in the theme song. Our Rachel and Monica though, their theme song would be, "We'll have sex with you, as long as you have money, We'll have sex with you, just buy us some clothes." I laughed as I thought about it. I then watched the episode where Chandler and Joey won Rachel and Monica's apartment in a bet about who knew each other better.

A few more days had passed and Markus was beginning to talk to me again. Markus told me that the past year was the best year of his life, and like all good times, they moved too fast. He talked about the daze he was in, and how for the first time since he began working at age fourteen, he didn't have any worries until now. I had to agree, it was the way life was supposed to be, and now it was over. He said that deep down he knew it was too good to be true. He thanked me for letting him be a part of everything.

It was then that I discovered that maybe, just possibly the good times didn't have to end. We were sitting in the kitchen, I was getting ready to go for one of my last annual swims in the only underground pool I will probably ever own. Markus was just getting out of the pool and had a towel wrapped around his head as we were talking.

"You know, we don't have to go backwards," I said.

"What do you mean?" Markus asked.

"Well, suppose we didn't work," I said.

"I don't get it, how would we pay for stuff?" Markus asked.

"Suppose we didn't buy stuff," I said.

"OK, just tell me what you mean," Markus said.

"What if we grew our own food? Built our own shelter?"

"You know anything about that?" Markus asked.

"No but we could find out," I replied.

"I don't know, how would we watch TV? Wouldn't we still need to pay for electricity?" Markus asked.

"Who says we need TV?" I replied.

"I do, I need TV," Markus stated.

"Hmm, I bet if you beg hard enough to Steve, he'll let you have your job back," I replied.

Markus sat there and let everything I said sink in a little deeper before he replied. He might have been dreading the collar and chain being put around his neck more than I was. Markus and I had about two hundred thousand dollars a piece in our bank accounts; the rest went to Bernice Earl. You should have seen the look on my accountant's face when I told him to give everything to Bernice Earl. He was a nice guy, he begged me to rethink my decision. I didn't, in fact I couldn't.

I moved back in with my parents and Markus got a nice little apartment in Indy for about a grand a month. We both had become realists. Even though the money that we had made both of us wealthy for the time being, we both knew that it was exactly that, the time being. We figured it would last us a few years if we both lived conservatively. Going back to work for us at this point was not an option, we had tasted the fruit of sitting on our asses for far too long, and we weren't turning back.

We needed help if we were truly going to undertake this, so we studied. We bought every book available on growing your own garden; we even paid a farmer to teach us all the essentials on growing our own vegetables. Me and Markus, both wondered how what we planted came to grow. We spent a few early mornings with just the farmer. He constantly chewed tobacco and when he would spit, he would inadvertently spit on his plants. He was one of those good-old-boy types. He knew what he was doing though; he had a few acres of plants, from corn to beans to squash.

Me and Markus particularly wanted to learn how to grow carrots, cabbage and potatoes. Over the years, me and Markus had grown fond of my mother's cabbage stew. The farmer recommended we buy some cattle from him, having a few to milk, and having a few to slaughter. I was absolutely against this, but knew that for this to work out, we needed to eat.

Markus and I weren't quite sure where we were going to achieve all this. We knew that we wanted a secluded area, away from the rest of the world but close enough so we could get to it if we wanted to. We knew this place existed somewhere, but didn't know exactly where it was.

We both had become dependent on TV throughout our lives and knew that for us to survive on our own, we couldn't look to TV to entertain us anymore. It wasn't exactly that it cost money for the electricity, but more that the influences it had on us caused us to feel like we needed to buy the various things it advertised. We knew that we couldn't do this anymore. We both had strictly turned ourselves off television as we prepared to leave the society we didn't want to be a part of anymore, until one day I cheated.

I was bored. My parents were at the office, curing people, and I was sitting on the most expensive couch health insurance could buy. I turned on the television, I noticed Billy Murray's familiar face, and noticed the name of the movie was Caddyshack. Now, I had never seen Caddyshack. For some reason I don't think I was meant to until that moment arose. Caddyshack? I said to myself. For some reason this meant something to me, but for the life of me I couldn't figure out what it was. I just sat there on the couch, thinking 'Caddyshack'? What is that? Why does that sound familiar, then suddenly, it came to me. That was it, it was perfect.

The Caddyshack was the cabin I found on the way back from getting tested for AIDS. Now, I hadn't seen the log cabin with the missing letter 'C' titled "addyshack" in the daytime, but that was soon to change. I got on the phone and told Markus that I was picking him up tomorrow morning. I finally figured out why I drove down that long dirt road and I couldn't wait to get there to see it again. I picked Markus up bright and early and we got to the "Addyshack" in about three hours. Markus didn't say much at first glance of the place, but he was soon looking for a good place to plant vegetables. From that point I took it that the place would do.

It was noon and the sunlight drifting through the tree branches lit up the "Addyshack." There was a hole in the roof from a large tree branch that had fallen on it. It probably happened from a storm. On the inside you could tell that at one time a happy little family had used this cabin for camping. I imagined the kids got older, or a divorce loomed. Either way the kids' old Tonka trucks and GI Joes hadn't been touched since probably nineteen ninety-five. There was a nice large portrait from the mannerism period next to the squeaky front door, but it was severely damaged from the rain. There were some nice clothes drawers and two beds that were still covered by half of the roof and weren't severely damaged enough to be thrown out like mostly everything else.

First off, me and Markus wanted to purchase the place, it seemed like that would possibly be difficult since we had no idea where to even begin with that one. The Addyshack was out in the middle of nowhere, which was perfect, but it also made it hard to find the owner. Me and Markus stayed at a hotel on a highway not too far away. The next two days we spent the mornings cleaning the place up, then we spent the evenings wondering what the hell we were doing, the place wasn't ours yet. It seemed to be a bit of boredom and anticipation for yet another new life.

The closest neighbor to the Addyshack was about twenty miles. It was a farm, and me and Markus had little doubt that the farm's owner even knew about the Addyshack. Me and Markus were standing outside on the farmer's porch as we knocked on the door and waited for an answer. This was the third time we had done this, and yet, there was still no answer. Markus sat on the farmer's rickety porch swing and said.

"We put in enough work at that place already, we should just claim it the way it is." I looked at Markus with wonder.

"What do you mean?" I said. Markus looked back as he swung back and forth.

"No one has been there for at least ten years, if worse comes to worse, and we still can't find anyone who knows anything, we could always just move in anyways. It's not like that place is worth anything. I mean, the property maybe is but it's not like we won't be able to afford it."

When me and Markus first thought of living off the fruits of our own labor, little did we know that it would suck extremely bad. It's hard for anyone to really get a good grasp of it. Maybe the hardest day working at the maternal clothing store for me and Markus combined, then multiplied by two, and it still didn't cut it. What eventually happened was that me and Markus did move into the Addyshack, we paid a few construction guys who seemed to know what they were doing to put a proper roof on the cabin.

Me and Markus worked, worked, and worked to put the place together. It was always something. Something always needed done. We worked, worked, and worked some more. I would keep myself going by telling myself that it would soon be done, soon the Addyshack would be livable, then we worked, worked, and worked some more. I sweated my balls off every day, till one day I got to the point that I had to ask Markus if we did the right thing. Markus laughed and then assured me that we were about done.

I hadn't noticed it, but Markus had become the leader in our two-man army. He was the boss, somehow Markus had become the leader and I had become the peasant. It kind of irritated me; I suppose that things work themselves out like that naturally. Naturally someone has to lead and someone has to follow.

Me and Markus plowed and planted some vegetables, we did everything right, we watered them we treated them; we took care of them as if we birthed them. We would take turns pulling weeds, and then somehow always inevitably, the plants died. Oh yeah, and our cow we bought, forget about it. We named her Sue, neither of us had the heart to milk the damn thing let alone slaughter it. We spent a few weeks putting up fences; apparently Sue's favorite food was the vegetables me and Markus couldn't keep alive. We had chickens in a makeshift fence we built, they too became pets, and we named them as well. It was much easier to drive an hour and forty minutes to the KFC, pick up a bucket of chicken and some groceries. Our garden sure wasn't satisfying our stomachs.

Because of boredom and our starving bellies, we started getting to know a few of the girls at the local bar. Sometimes we'd drive to our place where we would have a little bit of a get together, and then we would wake up around noon and do it all over again. We were definitely squandering our opportunity at never having to work at a shitty job again. I wasn't very good at deterring Markus either; the first three months were embarrassing. We'd try to get work done around the cabin, but we were mostly hung over, and the work was so god damn hard. Markus was starting to get better with the plants though; he eventually had our small garden picked clean of weeds. I sometimes would sit from the porch and watch, I felt like a dipshit when I woke one morning to find him burning all the weeds he had picked from the night before.

Soon after, Markus grew his first tomato. We split it; it was thrilling that we had actually accomplished this. We started to get a better hang on things. Markus showed me some of the tools he had picked up from trial by error on the tomatoes, I used the things he taught me and grew a patch of my own.

We would joke about eating Sue, our cow. The truth was that Sue had become the third member of our Addyshack society. Sometimes she would make her way into the cabin if we left the door open on a hot Sunday evening and me and Markus would have to usher her out the best we could. Usually the corn that we grew and had forbid her of eating did the trick.

It was beginning to get cold; frost was starting to land on the grass in the morning as winter was coming. Me and Markus didn't have enough vegetables to stock up for winter since we had so much trouble at the beginning of the planting season. Markus and I decided that we would have to give in and buy our own food from the market to make it through the winter. The Addyshack cabin didn't really fight off the cold breezes as well as we would have liked, you could always hear the wind make its way through the cabin. Most days I was covered in blankets tightly wrapped around my body and head. Markus had become more intense as the winter thickened, as if he was worried, as if his survival instincts kicked in.

It was too cold for me to be going around throwing fits about work like Markus, so I let Markus work and I watched most of the time. He was so goddamn worried; it did him good to get rid of all that energy. There was nothing to worry about in my mind because I had a Hummer. The Army used Hummers; it could plow through anything if we needed it to. Markus would just go on and on, it was always something with him. He'd put his hands on his hips, frown at the sight of us getting snowed in, and then start in again about if we had enough food or not.

This one particular day things were different, it was too cold and the banging of Markus's hammer for the last hour was starting to drive me insane.

"Markus, can you give the hammer a break!?" I yelled. Markus came out of my bedroom where he was nailing up plaster over the installation to keep the cold breezes from coming in my room.

"Are you gonna do any work? Ever? Or just get by letting me do everything?" I turned around from sitting on the couch as best I could with blankets restricting my movement and said, "I told you, Markus, I will do my own room, just focus on yours!"

Markus snapped back, "Mine's done. Meanwhile it's been two months since you said you would do yours, and I still feel the cold breezes coming through your room and into mine."

Irritated, I replied, "It has not been two months! It's been a few weeks!"

Marcus and I had been fighting like a married couple for the last few months, and the fight about the installation seemed to be going on forever.

"There's nothing to even do all day, what do you do all day that requires your time? Nothing! You just sit around moping all the time," Markus replied.

"I think, Markus, OK? Sorry that I use something other than my cock."

"Oh right, I forgot, you're smarter than me."

Markus walked away back into my bedroom where he continued to hammer. I don't know why, but Markus was also on a kick about me thinking I was smarter than him. I mean, I was but I never voiced that opinion out loud, there was no reason to throw a fuss about it.

Since we didn't have any electricity, I usually just charged my cell phone in the Hummer. I did the night before, I don't know why since I didn't receive many phone calls. My cell phone rang. I picked it up; it was the slimy, cheating publishing company. I guess the small royalty checks had been building up. Normally I wouldn't have cared or I would have just told them to send them to Bernice's address, but I desperately needed to get out of the Addyshack cabin. This was the perfect excuse.

I drove two or three hours and arrived in a sweatshirt and jeans. My hair and beard had grown like a mountain man and I was barely recognizable to some, but others knew who I was, at least I hoped. The secretary was one.

"Haven't seen you in awhile," she stated.

"Yep, just up to no good as usual," I replied.

She smiled and handed me the envelopes. "Here they are."

"Thanks," I replied. I began to walk away, and thought to myself that I would have a small meal somewhere nice; I was tired of eating corn. This would have really pissed off Markus if he knew I was eating at a buffet somewhere. I smiled as I walked away, thinking to myself about pancakes or waffles. Of course, something disturbing had to break my train of thought, as a happy little moment seems to never last. Thinking about it now, I wish that the secretary would have just shut her fucking mouth and never said anything. She should've just gone back to filing papers, or doing whatever the hell they normally do. But she couldn't, the universe had seen a moment of happiness, and it had to be ruined.

The secretary yelled with my back towards her. "Hey! Remember that woman that was in here?"

"Yeah? Why?" I asked.

"Well, I just wanted you not to worry about her, she's no relation to Oliver." The secretary smiled, perky like, and went back to typing.

My jaw dropped and I slowly walked back to the secretary's desk like a pissed off Freddy Kruger.

"What do you mean? No relation?" I asked.

"Bob checked her out, she's this insane con artist, and Bob said she's even been hospitalized a few times for actually thinking she was people she wasn't. We think she read about your story in the newspaper and tried to come up with some scheme to weasel out money." I couldn't quite grasp what she had just said, and could only shake my head.

"Whoa, whoa, whoa, you're just telling me this now?"

Her face looked perplexed, curious, as to why I was asking. She had no idea what I had done and neither did anyone else.

"Yeah, no one wanted to trouble you until they got the facts. Actually I wasn't even supposed to tell you about her, is there something wrong?" she asked.

I couldn't believe it. I had acted on impulse, I was took. I believed Bernice's story, if that's even her real name. The embarrassment couldn't bring myself to say anything; I was more concerned with pummeling Bernice's face. I walked hurriedly out the publishing company doors. I quickly started thinking about how this could've happened as I drove frantically, speeding like I had never speeded before.

I got out of my Hummer, walking fast with my head up, ready for a fight. I ran up the steps to Bernice's house and knocked on the door. The door swung open, as it was unlocked. I walked in to find an empty house. I walked into the living room where only the walls heard the tall stories that were told to me, not knowing if any of it was actually true. A stunned feeling came over me, I started to feel like I was going to faint, so I sat down on the barren floor. Suddenly I started to hear movement, the movement started coming down the stairs, I rose with anticipation. It was a white woman with a business suit, along with a black couple looking at the house for the first time. The white woman saw me and reacted in panic mode, as she knew I wasn't supposed to be in the house.

"Excuse me, may I help you?" she asked.

Yes you can, I thought, you can help me get my million dollars back, you can help me get my house with the underground pool back, and you can help me find the woman who conned me and put her to death by way of electrocution. I could've said any of that, and maybe this woman could've helped in some way. Maybe, just maybe, she knew the whereabouts of the woman who once lived there and who called herself Bernice. Maybe the publishing company could've even helped, maybe contacting the police, the FBI or even the National Guard could've helped. All of it was just one more reason that I realized I was better off where I currently was, away, away from people who are constantly trying to hurt each other. I was too shocked and stunned at the moment to say anything.

I left Bernice's empty house with the intention to never return. I never did. It was nice while it lasted, and maybe the little con needed the money more than me, my guess was that even if I had spent the time and the effort of tracking her down, the money would have never been recovered. It had been months, and the money was long gone, spent on ridiculous lavish jewelry, trips around the world, and toys, expensive useless toys. I knew that at that moment she was right back where I was, working, or trying to con someone else with whatever elaborate scheme she could come up with next, someone who was smarter than I was, someone who would put her in jail. Either way, she existed on borrowed time.

The sun had fallen and darkness had risen by the time I got back to the Addyshack. I knew that Markus could hear nothing of my journey. He would have killed me if I had strolled in and told him. The deep pain I had felt, the pain that I thought was the rest of the world coming down on me, was gone when I was at the Addyshack. Being with the dead tree bark of the winter and the cold dirt begging for sunlight had made me forget what it was like being threatened by the ways of the world. This was normally when I was alone though, just me and in the middle of nature with the Addyshack.

Then Markus would come around, he had gotten in really good shape the last few months. I mean, he was naturally in good shape, but from doing the majority of the yard work and out of boredom doing push-ups and sit-ups everyday, he had grown into quite the Greek statue. His demeanor had changed towards me, as if he resented me, I think this happens normally when you're around the same person twenty-four hours a day. Markus, over the months and even more so as days went on, had begun to become very intent on making me pitch in more than usual. I'll be the first to admit that the surroundings we lived in caused me to have more of a wandering mind, I'd see a flower lose its peddles in the wind and I'd be off in another land.

Markus was starting to get aggressive with me, and I had changed more and more over the months. I had become completely weak at any thought towards confrontation. Markus had grown almost opposite of me. The land and cabin that he tended, and tended well I might add, had made him the way I once was. He seemed to hate everything and not know why. Now, I wasn't forcing him to stay, he could've left and went back. I honestly started to wonder what he was doing anymore.

It was morning in the middle of a snowy winter. I had gotten up early to pick up wood for the fireplace. I had decided to see if Markus wanted to come too but as I peeked in his room I noticed that he was in one of his very deep sleeps, mouth open, head falling off the bed. I picked up some spare wood and cut some branches down; as I did I heard our cow moo loudly. This was common, as she would always make a ruckus once she knew we were up in the morning so that we would feed her. I smiled thinking about her waiting on me to feed her. We, or should I say Markus, had built a shelter for her so that she would have a place to go in the breezy cold. I collected the branches for the fireplace and walked up through the snow and out of the woods to the Addyshack.

I headed toward Sue's shelter where I called out "Sueeeeeeeeee!" Usually she gave out a big moo, as she had gotten to know her name. This time she didn't, and as I got closer I realized that she never would again. I had gotten about fifteen feet away when I noticed blood soaking the snow and seeping out of her small shelter. Before I could get there Markus had came around and went into the shelter with blood on his coat.

"Markus?!" I screamed. He said nothing back. As I got closer I saw Markus kneeling down next to Sue, gutting her from neck to stomach. "What the fuck is going on, Markus?!" Markus didn't even bother to turn around as if he hadn't done a thing.

"Were out of hamburger and I don't feel like driving all day to get it."

It was yet another time where I didn't believe that the incidents of the day had actually happened. I wanted to cry, I wanted to shout, and most of all I wanted to fucking kill Markus. I had never gotten this feeling before, not even from smashing the alcohol bottle on that poor kid's face. This was something else. I couldn't move, I could only watch as Markus gutted Sue and let her blood drain. I wanted to leave and destroy my cheeks with fallen tears, but I felt that if I had moved at all, I would have took Markus's knife and gutted him. Every inch of my being was aching to do it. A deep dark rage had settled in.

I swiftly turned away and walked furiously back into the house. I walked into my room and wept with anger like I had never done before. I could only beat up my old wobbly dresser drawer. My teeth ground with every punch and kick I gave it. Markus had must have walked in without me noticing as he opened my bedroom door. He gave me a look of no remorse and snickered. I was about to rip his nostrils off and feed them to him, it all depended on his next move. He laughed as he saw a tear of anger come down my face.

"What's the matter? You crying like a baby 'cause your pet cow's dead?" He laughed again.

I clinched my fist and growled with anger. I couldn't hold it in; I was foaming at the mouth. I smashed his dipshit face harder than I'll ever punch again. He fell out of my room and I jumped on him with all my anger and ferociously continued punching. I was too mad, and at this point so was Markus as I stood over him and punched him again and again. But Markus wasn't so steamed that he couldn't think like I was. Markus went from laying on the ground, grabbed my leg and flipped me upside down and stood up himself.

The next few minutes are unclear to me, I don't remember feeling anything, I just saw an unfocused Markus standing over me and continually punching me. I woke up bloody and still on the floor of the cabin. The next thirty minutes were a daze, as all I could do was just lay there and try to compose myself. Every bone in my body ached, especially the bones in my face. Markus's door was shut as I presumed that's where he was. I went into the bathroom and checked my face on our old scratched up dusty mirror. My face was so swollen I looked like the elephant man. A huge knot was on the right side of my face; I assumed this was because Markus was left-handed. My nose was definitely broken. I was given an Owen Wilson nose at the hands of Markus. Maybe it would bring me some bikini models, too.

What didn't make sense to me was how Markus couldn't have given a damn about our cow. Maybe he wanted to hurt me, but even so, how could he do it at the expense as something so innocent and loving? I'm someone who can't cry at a human being's funeral, not family, and not friends. When a human being dies, to me it's almost like they finally got what they deserved after all those years of cruelty to other fellow mankind, and in Markus's case, animal kind. Markus was beginning to be just like I once was, someone who didn't care about anyone or anything. I had never sunk as deep as Markus though, to kill something so innocent. It wasn't possible for me. I think maybe he needed the structure in his life, he needed someone telling him what to do, he needed to be a slave for some millionaire.

I, on the other hand, had felt like I changed for the better, but for my progress to continue, I decided right then and there that I had to leave Markus. Our friendship was done in my eyes. I couldn't ever be close to someone who resembled the old me any longer. I decided that I would find a place similar to the Addyshack and call it my own.

Over the next few days there was tension, me and Markus didn't speak, we both tried to stay out of each other's way the best we could. I had gotten over being angry, but was pretty distraught about what had happened to our cow. I had slept in one morning and woke up to the smell of hamburger. I didn't leave my room that day. I could hear Markus looking for the salt and pepper though. He had reminded me to get some from the store the last two times I went. I always forgot. I decided that I wouldn't come up with some big speech, or basically think of anything to say to Markus at all, he didn't deserve that. I was going to leave and that would be it. Have a good life, I would say, and hopefully I would never see him again, I thought.

I had all my stuff together from the night before, Markus was playing himself in chess and could visibly see that I was packing up my stuff. He didn't say anything. I figured it was his ploy to pretend he didn't care what I did. This made me angrier for some reason. I began moving quicker and before I knew it I had packed everything I owned into the Hummer. In the heat of the moment, I decided that Markus didn't even deserve a "have a good life" comment. I climbed into the Hummer like a fifteen-year-old girl mad at her father. I took one last look at the Addyshack, looked at my swollen face in the rearview mirror, and turned the ignition... nothing. I turned the ignition again, and still nothing.

Now, I'm by no means a man's man, when it comes to vehicles, but I decided to lift the hood anyways. The engine looked normal to me but I'm not a mechanic at all. I was starting to sweat as I tried to think what it could be. The ignition was silent; I would try it again and again, still nothing. I sat in the driver's seat with frustration as I took time to man up and ask Markus for help. Markus wasn't a mechanic either but he knew how to fix cars from his days of driving junkers around. I walked in and Markus was still sitting there, playing chess.

"Can you do me a favor and see what's wrong with the Hummer?" I asked.

Markus was silent, not looking at me, and then he uttered, "It's broke."

"Yeah, I know the Hummer's broke, I've been trying to start it for the last fifteen minutes," I replied.

"You plan on going somewhere, Richard?" Markus asked.

"Yeah, I plan on going home, now can you fix the Hummer?"

Markus had been getting stranger and stranger, but I hadn't ever seen him like this. Markus looked up very slowly. "You never asked me if you could leave," Markus said.

I squinted at him, trying to understand what he meant by that. I was convinced that he couldn't hear what I was saying, so I walked closer, my back lowered towards him so he could better understand.

"Uhh, I'm leaving, Markus. I'm gonna find my own place, you understand me?"

Markus very sternly and sharply pounded his bloody bandaged fist on the table. "You're not going to be the head nigger in charge of me any longer! You're gonna do your share around here or I'll beat it out of you!" Markus pointed at me with anger in his eyes.

He couldn't be serious, I thought to myself, but if he was, he was really, really, pissing me off. I walked closer, face to face with him now as he stood up. "You got fucking lucky last time, you're lucky I didn't pulverize your ass. If you wanna still be breathing in the next ten seconds, you'll get out there and fix that Hummer," I told him.

I was so angry my knee began wobbling. As I think back on it now, I was more nervous than angry. What I said was bullshit; I knew Markus could beat my ass again if he wanted to. I wasn't about to let him keep me there, though. I might have told you before about our so-called survival training. The farmer had given us a rifle for hunting, but since me and Markus were both bad shots, and the fact that I just couldn't bring myself to shoot something so harmless and innocent as an animal, it never got used. What I didn't see during our conversation was that the rifle had been laying up against Markus's leg. He made sure I saw it after my last comment. If I had seen it sooner, I would have known that Markus was completely off his rocker.

I stood back and said, "OK, Markus, OK, fine, have it your way." I backed up all the way to the door of my room, almost hitting it. I went through my bedroom door and closed it as Markus sat down. I knew that I wasn't going to be having any shuteye that night. I sat next to my bed most of the night and smoked cigarettes out the window, waiting for an opportune time for Markus to enter his room and doze off. I sat and waited, sat and waited, and sat and waited some more.

It was about three AM. It had finally been a reasonable amount of time where Markus hadn't made any noise. I peeked through the door; Markus wasn't anywhere to be seen. I opened the door and his door was shut, he had snuck into his room without me hearing him. I wasn't exactly looking forward to the walk, but it had to be done, I went out the door very carefully so that the door wouldn't squeak. I left all my possessions in the Hummer, and began to make the walk out of the woods. I figured it would probably take a few hours before I got to the main road. I never got the chance to see. Once I hit the open stretch towards the woods, I began to swiftly walk. I had walked maybe a few minutes before Markus appeared behind me with the rifle pointed right at the back of my head.

"Richard!" Markus yelled. I turned around and I knew that Markus's brain had officially left the building and was nowhere to be found. I raised my hands very calmly and collectively; I didn't want to have any more aggressive talk with Markus.

"Markus? What are you doing?" I asked.

"Get back in the cabin," Markus told me.

"Put the gun down. Come on, Markus, this is stupid," I said.

"You're trying to leave me here so that I'll do everything. It's not going to happen, Richard," Markus said.

Markus might've been going apeshit, but under no circumstances could I ever imagine Markus shooting anyone. I had known him all my life; he just wasn't capable of doing it. It wasn't in him. I figured I could slowly talk him down and still get to the main road by sunrise.

"Markus, you don't want to-" And BAM! Just like that, the trigger had slipped I thought as I ducked down. I rose back up with my ears ringing, more pissed than anything since he had so dumbfoundedly let his finger slip.

"Markus!" I yelled. I looked at him and he didn't have the royal fucked-up look I thought he would have. He had more of an intentional look in his eyes. I noticed that the barrel of the rifle had been pointing down as Markus let the gun fall next to his leg. He looked down towards the lower half of my body with a serious gaze. I followed that gaze to my feet. I hadn't felt a thing, but once I looked down and saw my right leather shoe torn to bits with blood seeping out. I shrieked. The pain had hit me about three times more than when I broke my thumb throwing baseballs in Little League. Up to that point, that had been the most painful moment of my life.

I lowered my body to hold my foot as I shrieked and spit in pain. The calmness toward Markus had ended as I cursed him with every dirty word in the book.

You see, the problem with my life was that the agony came from non-penetrative bullets, and of all times, I get this revelation now, when an actual real bullet entered my foot. All I could do was scream. After about a minute of screaming, Markus held the gun to my head, and made me limp back to the Addyshack.

He took me to my room where he handcuffed my left hand to the bedpost. When and where he got the handcuffs were beyond me, probably from one of his numerous sex toy bags. If he had been planning this for a week, a month, or even longer, was even more beyond me. I had no idea what his intentions were, and frankly, I had no idea what his intentions could be. He was pissed I knew that, but so was I. I was very compliant after he shot me in the foot; I let him handcuff me and tried not to weep like a baby.

At some point, I cried myself to sleep but woke up the next morning still in agonizing pain. I woke up, screaming at the top of my lungs. Markus swung the door open and gave me some pills and water. From my small experience with pharmaceutical drugs, it was Vicodin, and three sure did the trick. I felt like things were going to be OK, every few hours Markus would come in and give me another dose.

"Where'd you get these?" I asked.

"You remember last year when we would take 'em to get through our family Christmases?"

"Yeah," I said.

"I never stopped," Markus said.

Markus took me at gunpoint to look for wood for the fire. We walked into the woods and I asked him straightforward what he was thinking the moment we went out the door. "Are you going to shoot me out here or something?" I asked.

"If I have to, don't make me have to," Markus said.

"Why are you doing this?" I asked.

"It's too late for me, Rich," Markus said.

Now, Markus's health had been deteriorating, but I had been so absorbed in myself that I hadn't noticed. I couldn't comprehend it at the time.

"What are you talking about? You look fine," I stated.

Markus glanced back at me with a serious look. "I'm done, Rich, I'm done."

I saw it in his eyes, I knew that he was telling the truth, and maybe this had contributed to his radical behavior. It must have. I felt for him, but this was ridiculous. Thankfully, he didn't shoot me again. I collected the wood and then he cuffed me back up to the bed.

Markus kept me cuffed to the bed for about three weeks, my beard had grown quite long and springtime had broke the grueling cold. Markus seemed to be in a rut as far as the regular routine went. Every morning he'd wake me up and uncuff me at gunpoint, and then we would have breakfast where he would lay the gun up against himself, or sometimes up against a chair next to him. The conversation was always stale as I just tried to comply as best I could; our friendship was far-gone at this point.

After breakfast he would usher me around as I did various things around the Addyshack. I'd feed the chickens, some sheep that he later slaughtered, then I would do what was needed to be done around the Addyshack, and it seemed like there was always something that needed to be done.

I began to understand what drove Markus so crazy about me not pitching in. One day it was the chicken fence; the chickens had found an escape route. I had to run around catching them and then patch up the hole. Then there was cleaning out the shelter for the sheep, they had used the same place they slept in as a toilet during the winter, and it had gotten so bad that they couldn't use the shelter anymore. It took hours to dig the shit out of the place. One day it was the Addyshack roof needed fixed, the next he had me fill the installation in the walls, I didn't quite understand what Markus was gaining from all this. Every day there seemed to be something that needed done.

Markus would smoke a cigarette or two as he bossed me around and made sure I did everything right according to his standards. His standards had grown quite exhausting. Still I just didn't get it, and finally as I was putting the installation in the walls, I had to ask.

"You plan on keeping things like this forever, Markus?"

Markus was sitting in a rocking chair with the rifle and a cigar. "I hadn't really thought it all the way through, I guess I'll have to kill you, won't I?" Markus asked.

I smirked to myself that he thought he could intimidate me; he had to know that I would eventually escape. Some of the time Markus would be drunk; the mixture with the Vicodin which I assumed he was still taking would have him swaying a bit. These times would have been opportune if he hadn't grown so angry at every swig. He'd hold the barrel of the gun to my head and rattle off the ABC's, he would always cock the gun between P and Z, and I have no idea why. I began to realize he was toying with me, and the fear that he would strike in me from doing these things made him stronger, but just eventually ran dull on me.

I had gotten to a point where I wasn't limping as bad, it was time to make a break for it, I thought. I didn't know when or how. Every once in a while he would leave an opportunity for me wide open. A few times he had turned his back on me when we were in the woods to take a piss. My foot was in too bad shape then and I wouldn't have gotten far, but now, now I felt like I could maybe lose myself in the woods. I saw that as the mistake I made last time, trying to escape down the road instead of through the woods. I thought a few times about breaking something over his head when he made me do the dishes, but he always carried that rifle with him, it wasn't ever more than a few feet away. If I didn't knock him out on the first impact, I had to assume he would have killed me. That's what he was leading me to believe, anyways.

Every day was some kind of new mind fuck. It wasn't enough that he had me doing all the work around the house, but he had to intimidate me as well. Sometimes, not all the time, it would just make me angry. Certain things he did, like in the mornings when I would grab the eggs from the chicken hens, I hated doing this because the chickens would peck my hand. I did it slower than Markus did, I guess this irritated him, the chicken pecks would sometimes make me bleed though, so I would continue to go at my own pace.

Then one day Markus picked up our deflated football that we had at the house and launched it at my head. It struck my forehead, and boy what I would have done just for him to leave that rifle behind for just two seconds. It began to be an ordinary routine; I would go under the hens, grab the eggs, and he would launch whatever he could find at my head. I eventually got to the speed he liked, I felt like I was robbing a bank the way I was moving so fast.

By the time we had eaten a meal that he made me cook, I was so tired I didn't care if I was handcuffed or not. He always did, but I was so exhausted that didn't matter, I slept and slept, till morning anyways, then he would wake me up and we would follow the same routine. Saturday and Sunday he would leave me handcuffed, as he would take the Hummer into the city for food, I realized that the Hummer wasn't that broke at all, it was probably something simple that he did in five seconds.

My favorite was when he would uncuff me to go the bathroom, I'd have to holler to wake him up, and he'd carry a hatchet in and uncuff me. A hatchet, like he was a murderer or something. I didn't know why I hadn't taken this as serious as I should have, maybe because I had known him for so long. All I knew was that he had shot me once and seemed to want to shoot me again.

It had been maybe another month or two of this, all I remember was that it was spring, and that it was planting season. For the first time he had gave me something I could do some damage with, a hoe. He had me digging up the dirt in straight lines back and forth for about a third of an acre. Markus was off to the side with a straw hat and the rifle, he was sitting on a lawn chair coughing up something awful, he had grown really pale and thin. I didn't know why and didn't care at this point. Now, usually he would keep his fear mongering not personal, and at times more ludicrous than anything else. But for some reason on this day, he must've really had a problem with me, or maybe it was just himself he had a problem with. I figured he had to be feeling pretty down on himself with all this, and the drinking definitely wasn't helping.

I was hoeing the dirt away, sighing as the sun hit my face, wiping the sweat from my forehead with my sleeve. Markus was murmuring something to himself, or to me, I couldn't really tell, the noise of dirt flinging up in the air made me unable to hear. I was just trying to get through the day, bide my time till an opportunity arose, when before I knew it, Markus was right on top of me.

"What's your problem, you can't hear?!" Markus yelled.

Markus swiped the hoe from my grip and threw it on the ground. I stood there, not letting his behavior get to me as he walked back to the lawn chair and sat down.

"I thought you wanted to get this done today?" I asked. Markus took a swig of his whiskey and wiped his mouth. He was drunk and angry as usual.

"I told you to stop hoeing for a second, you dumb ass!"

I kept quiet as I awaited some more lashing. Markus was more drunk than usual at this point. There was a silence as I waited, almost as if he was contemplating what he should say next. He then uttered something that would ultimately determine the rest of his life, and that's the reason I think I decided to share all this.

"You know what you and that hoe have in common?" Markus slurred.

I looked at the hoe in the dirt, as I was about to hear something different for a change. He took a big swig from the bottle, his head swayed and his eyes were glazed.

"You both like dirt."

I smirked at his drunkenness. "Wow, Markus, good one. Why don't you sober up, take five minutes, think of a good one, and get back to me?" I grabbed the hoe and began digging.

"Hey, I thought of one," Markus then stated.

"Oh yeah? What's that?" I asked enthusiastically.

"You know when I fucked Veronica with you that night?" I immediately stopped what I was doing and slowly turned my head towards Markus. "Let's just say it wasn't the first time."

Markus grinned from ear to ear with this remark. I could tell that Markus was hoping to hurt me, he was waiting for a reaction, a twitch, a storm of rage, anything. I just stood there, looking at his dumb face, hoping by chance that it would instantly explode. Markus tilted his head with his little smirk then uttered, "Just about every time you left us alone, I'd have her little polka dot panties around her ankles."

It felt like my skin was going to turn inside out, or my insides were going to combust. Markus then leaned forward.

"What's the matter, you gonna cry? You gonna cry like when I tore open your stupid little cow? Come on, cry for me. Veronica sucked good cock, she couldn't wait most times for you to leave us alone together."

I went back to hoeing, back and forth, harder and faster as Markus's voice began to fade out as he continued barrage me with comments, I continued to bide my time as he continued to drink and try to get a reaction. Before long the bottle of whiskey was gone, Markus had given up trying to chastise me, and then before much longer, he had made the biggest mistake of his life, he fell asleep.

The sun was baking him brown on the lawn chair, with the cowboy hat nearly over his eyes. I wanted him to be awake for what I was about to do; I wanted him to feel what I felt. I took his rifle and threw it on the ground; he didn't deserve an easy way out. I stood above him with the dirt-clotted hoe. I felt like God. The sun was piercing, causing both of us to sweat. His mouth was open, as the liquor had caused him to doze off completely like a baby. I could feel the hate in my eyes for him beaming out; I bit my lip, as almost to hold back, it was quite the sight he must have seen.

"Hey, Markus!" I yelled. Markus's eyes opened and I swung, without a question of right or wrong, without aiming, I cut his head like a watermelon. I caught him square between the mouth. The hoe stuck to the inside of his throat. He was still alive, and his head was halfway severed. I dug my foot into his chest and began to yank out the hoe. There was little movement; all he did was groggle and panic. With a little more force the hoe was dislodged. Blood began falling from his mouth like a waterfall.

It was if he was suddenly mentally ill, this image still haunts me to this day. I will never understand it, the hoe hadn't entered his brain, but his eyes and face were squirming. It was if he wanted to move but couldn't. I stood there looking at him; there was no sense of guilt, no remorse. I was just perplexed by the way his body was reacting. I picked the hoe up over my head and swung it again, this time directly into his brain. His blood hit my face like confetti; he was still alive and convulsing more rapidly.

I dug my foot into his chest again. I pulled the hoe from his head and by this time his head and his shoulders were completely drenched with blood. I couldn't understand why he was still alive, so I continued, again and again until he finally stopped moving. The clotted dirt on the hoe was now in his mouth and inside his head. I stood there, out of breath, I dropped the hoe and picked up the rifle, almost as if I was scared of him picking it up and shooting me.

I walked into the Addyshack bathroom where I could take a good look at myself. There was a bit of his brain and bone on my forehead. I took a towel and wiped my face. I felt nothing. I didn't feel free and I didn't feel sorry. Just nothing. I had thought that I would have felt better, or that at least I would have felt something.

I didn't change, I didn't take anything with me, I just walked about four or five hours out of the woods until I finally reached pavement. I walked down the side of the road without thinking of what I must of looked like. I started hailing down cars, and to my surprise a semi truck stopped. It was a truck driver about my dad's age. He asked me if I was OK. I had to think about it. I looked around and saw the beautiful open land.

"Yeah, I've set someone free."

www.ingramcontent.com/pod-product-compliance
Lightning Source LLC
Chambersburg PA
CBHW061136200626
46817CB00016B/1670